AF292151

Sins of the Shadow Walkers

A Familiar Curse Story by

C.L. Bright

Copyright © 2021 C.L. Bright
All rights reserved.
Cover Designed by J.N. Sheats
Proofreading by Kendra's Editing and Book Services

ISBN: 979-8-70-205848-1

The unauthorized reproduction or distribution of a
copyrighted work is illegal. Criminal copyright
infringement is investigated by federal law enforcement
agencies and is punishable by up to Five years in prison
and a fine of $250,000

Also by C.L. Bright

The Spellcaster's Trap
Beyond the Black Mist

Acknowledgments

I want to thank everyone who helped me with this new series. I really appreciate my daughters for inspiring me to take a chance with this genre. They have been asking me to write books they can read for the last couple of years. I also want to thank Levenia for being my sounding board as I built this new world. My beta readers, April, Kari, and Yvonne, are amazing and really helped me work out the final bugs in these books.

Thank you to my fabulous cover designer, J.N. Sheats, who is also an amazing author. Finally, thank you Kendra for catching my typos.

Chapter One

Juliet

The sunlight streaming through the window warmed me, and for a moment, I felt at peace. That feeling quickly faded, and I shot up in bed when I remembered the events of the previous day.

Sitting up so quickly was a mistake. I still felt dizzy and weak from whatever spell or drug had been used on me.

"You're finally awake."

My head turned in the direction of the male who'd spoken as my heart pounded against my ribs.

He was seated in the corner with his fingers steepled under his chin. He was tall with bronze skin, angular features, shoulder-length brown hair, and eyes the same shade of green as mine.

I'd seen him before. He was one of the Shadow Walkers who'd blocked my path to freedom.

"Can you talk?" he asked as he stood and moved closer, showing more concern than I'd have expected from a hunter. "Do I need to get a healer?"

I shook my head. "I can talk, and I don't need a healer."

He said nothing more as he studied me. "When

Nicolas Verdugo came to my father and asked if we had a witch named Juliet in our family, I didn't think anything of it, at least not until he described you and mentioned your eyes."

"I'm sure a lot of shapeshifters and spellcasters have green eyes," I pointed out.

"They do," he agreed. "The Shadow Walker eyes are quite distinctive. I was pretty sure it had to be you, though I still had some doubts."

"Can you tell me what's going on?" I asked. "You're being very cryptic, and you seem to know who I am while I have no clue who you are. Why did you kidnap me?"

"Kidnap you? I was rescuing you," he argued. "The fighting wasn't going well, so I got you out of there."

"Why?" I asked. "You're not only a spellcaster, your family hunts my kind. Why would you help me just because we have the same eyes?"

"I should probably introduce myself," he began. "I'm Kaine Shadow Walker, your uncle."

My mouth dropped open as I took in his words.

I wasn't a spellcaster. While I knew my father didn't tell me everything, he would have mentioned my mother being a spellcaster.

Yet, I still had doubts.

Had he lied to me?

No, it couldn't be true.

"That's not possible," I argued. "You can't be my uncle. You're a spellcaster."

"Like my sister, your mother," he stated. "I haven't seen her since shortly after her sixteenth birthday. That's when the whole world changed for us. I always hoped she'd try contacting me, but I suppose she's happier with her life among the shapeshifters."

"What you're saying isn't possible," I argued.

He let out a sigh. "I can't believe she never told you about me. I understand why your father never mentioned this side of your family. The others at the Heathergate Refuge would have never accepted his relationship with my sister if they'd known the truth, and they would also have an issue with your mixed heritage. I figured my sister would have told you. I thought that might have been why you claimed to be a Shadow Walker in Azuredale."

"My mother was from the Heathergate Refuge. Our leadership council would never have allowed my father to bring a hunter into our community," I pointed out. "Even unfamiliar shapeshifters aren't welcome."

My father had always been adamant about the dangers of welcoming any rebel shapeshifters, so I found it especially hard to believe he'd have brought a spellcaster in and made her his mate.

Keeping her identity as an outsider a secret wouldn't have been impossible. The Heathergate Refuge was big enough that a lot of families didn't know each other.

Those living in the outlying areas didn't interact with others, so my father could have convinced one of them to claim my mother as a member of their family. The leadership council would have been the hardest to fool, but it seemed my father had found a way.

"This is crazy," I whispered as I stood and walked toward the chest of drawers with the mirror on top.

My long black hair had been braided, though I didn't know by who, likely the same person who'd dressed me in soft gray pants and a matching shirt.

"Yes, it is," he agreed. "How is your mother?"

I turned to face him. "My mother died not long after my birth."

"I didn't know," he said softly. "I always pictured her living a long and happy life with your father. It made it easier to accept losing her."

"No, this can't be true," I argued. "My mother was a shapeshifter."

"Not exactly," he replied.

"What do you mean by *not exactly*? Either she was a shapeshifter, or she wasn't."

"This is a long story, and I think it would be best if we wait until after you've had something to eat."

"I don't need anything to eat. I need to know what's going on, and I need to get back to my friends. They could be in danger."

"They're fine," he assured me. "They made it into the Heathergate Refuge. I sent our cousin, Orlando, with a team to make sure nothing happened to them since I suspected you'd worry. He said there were a few Verdugos patrolling the area, but they'd seen no sign of your friends. It didn't sound like the Verdugos planned to remain in that area much longer, so your friends should be safe, even if they decide to leave the protected area."

"And I'm supposed to take your word for this?" I demanded. "How can I trust you?"

He shrugged. "You can't yet, but I hope that will change. Food?"

I shook my head. "I'll eat after you finish explaining to me what's going on."

He grinned. "You have the Shadow Walker stubbornness."

"Don't call me a Shadow Walker."

"But that's what you are," he stated.

I shook my head. "I'm a shapeshifter, not a spellcaster, and I'm certainly not a hunter."

"How about if we make a deal?"

"What kind of deal?" I asked.

"You can eat while I tell the story," he suggested.

I let out a frustrated breath. "Fine, you can talk while I eat."

My stomach was in knots, so I wasn't sure I could eat all that much, but it seemed I'd get more information if I stopped arguing.

He grinned. "See? We *can* compromise. I'll be back soon."

"Are you going to lock me in here?" I asked.

"No, and you're free to check the door after I leave if it will make you feel better."

Chapter Two

I waited a couple of minutes after he left the room before putting on my boots and hurrying to check the bedroom door. It wasn't locked, though I didn't know if that really mattered.

Would Kaine just let me leave? Or was this a trick to lull me into a false sense of security?

I'd heard that Tulurean homes were much smaller than those in Azuredale, so I didn't expect it to be hard to find an exit.

No one stopped me when I opened the door a crack. After looking down the empty corridor, I decided it might not be as easy to find the exit as I'd hoped.

The room I was in had a small but comfortable bed. The large window let in sunlight. It was nothing fancy, but still nice.

The hallway looked dank with gray walls and no windows. There were several closed doors; some appeared to have panels that opened to slide a tray through. My room might not look like a cell, but the corridor definitely looked like part of a prison.

I passed three doors before stopping in my tracks when I heard a male scream as if in excruciating pain.

When I took a step back, I ran into someone and spun,

ready to face an enemy.

The female behind me had long brown hair, green eyes like mine, and a slender build. She was taller than me and seemed familiar.

"You look like you can't decide if you should attack me, run, or introduce yourself," she said with a grin.

"I wasn't planning to introduce myself," I told her.

She laughed. "Then I guess it's good I already know who you are. I'm Calista."

"You were with Kaine the day he brought me back here," I replied.

She nodded. "He's my cousin, so I guess that makes you my cousin as well."

"I'm still not ready to believe that claim," I told her.

"I don't blame you," she replied.

Another scream from the cell made me cringe. "So, am I going to be tortured like the poor male you have in there?"

She quirked an eyebrow. "Poor male?"

"Whatever he's done, I doubt he deserves to be tortured," I told her.

"I disagree, but in this case, we aren't torturing anyone. He's being treated for injuries he sustained when he and Kaine fought. We should have let him die if you ask me."

"Why am I here?" I asked.

"You haven't spoken to Kaine yet?"

"He told me some crazy story about me being a Shadow Walker and then insisted on getting food for me before he'd tell me anything more. I can't see how any of this could be true."

She nodded. "I see why you feel that way. Your mother left before I was born, so I had a hard time believing the story, but I trust Kaine. That could be because he's the only one who stood up for me when I decided I wanted to be a healer instead of a hunter."

"Tulureans are allowed to make that kind of choice?" I asked.

"Not normally, and that's why Kaine's support meant so much," she explained. "He had enough pull to make it happen. I can't believe I'm finally meeting you."

"How long have you known about me?" I asked.

"Not long," she admitted. "I heard about you a little over a month ago, when Kaine asked for my help, but I've been dying to meet you since then."

There was another scream that made me cringe.

"You'll all die when my father finds out what you've done!"

My eyes narrowed as I walked closer to the cell. "Is that Nicolas?"

Calista followed me. "Yes, and he's the worst patient. I suppose I could have given him something for the pain, but he's lucky I gave him a healing spell at all after the horrible things he's threatened."

"You should have let him die," I said with no guilt.

Nicolas might be locked up now, but I didn't know how long that would last. I knew he'd be a problem for me as long as he lived.

"Juliet?"

I shuddered at the sound of his hoarse voice coming from the other side of the door.

"I know you're out there, Juliet."

"Yes, I'm out here while you're locked up," I replied with as much confidence as I could muster, considering I still didn't believe I wasn't also a prisoner.

"Don't trust them," Nicolas called out. "They're trying to use you because they know how powerful you are."

"And she should trust you?" Calista asked with a laugh.

"I don't trust either of you," I replied.

"That's smart," Calista agreed. "You don't know me, and I'm sure you know enough to say you can't trust Nicolas."

"Yes," I agreed loud enough for Nicolas to hear. "I definitely can't trust him."

"So, are you looking for a tour or seeing if you can find

your way out?" she asked.

"Seeing if I can find my way out," I replied. "Am I in a prison?"

"Yes, but you're staying in an unused guard's room," she explained. "Here, I'll show you the way out. It will probably make it easier to trust everything Kaine says when he gets back."

I nodded and walked beside her. "Are we on the Tulurgate Peninsula?"

"Yes, and that's why I don't recommend taking off on your own. It's not the safest place for you, but we figured there isn't any truly safe place."

"I'd have preferred to stay with my friends," I told her. "They need me."

"There was nothing you could have done for them after Nicolas knocked you out with that spell. They made it into the Heathergate Refuge, and they didn't come back out."

That made me worry even more.

Had shapeshifters attacked them on the other side?

Fiona and Darius had seen them fighting with me, and I'd told them Dante, Serena, and Geori were my friends. That didn't mean my father's guards hadn't assumed the worst when I was captured while my friends escaped.

"I have to get back to the Heathergate Refuge," I insisted.

"Tell that to Kaine," she replied as we reached the end of the corridor, and she pointed to the double doors. "You just have to walk through those doors to leave."

"What are you doing, Calista?" Kaine hissed as he approached us with a tray of food.

"Showing her the way out so she'll know she's not a prisoner," Calista explained.

"You thought you were a prisoner?" Kaine asked. "Even after I told you the door wasn't locked?"

"I am in a prison," I pointed out. "You're about to order me back to my cell, right?"

He sighed. "It's not a cell, and I'm not going to let you get yourself killed after all I did to save you."

"Kaine!"

He turned toward the male who'd just entered the building and then looked back at Calista. "Take her back to her room," he said urgently.

With no plan and a lot of questions, I decided it was best to follow Calista back to my room.

I could come up with a plan to leave later.

Chapter Three

I was still eating the bowl of soup from the tray when Kaine returned to my room.

He looked tired and irritated, but he smiled when he saw me eating.

"How do you like the soup?" he asked.

"It's very good," I replied honestly. "The spices in it are unlike anything I've had before."

He nodded. "We grow them here. This soup is one of my favorites. Your mother never cared for it."

At the reminder of his claim, I pushed the bowl to the side. "I've eaten enough. Tell me this story about how my mother was supposedly a Shadow Walker."

"For generations, there have been stories of spellcasters falling in love with familiars," he began. "Nearly all had horrific endings where the familiar turned on the spellcaster family and killed them."

"Scare tactics to give you another reason to keep your emotional distance from shapeshifters," I remarked.

He nodded. "Yes, that may be true. There were more romantic tales told in secret. My great-grandmother even had a journal with stories of a Shadow Walker who fell madly in love with a familiar. According to the story, Armand Shadow Walker broke every rule when he captured a beautiful familiar. Rather than turning her over, he brought her home with him, hiding her true identity and living happily ever after. There's more to the story, but those are the important details."

"Was there really a Shadow Walker by that name?" I asked.

He nodded. "Several generations back. Little is known about him. His witch was from a remote spellcaster community to the east, and they had five children."

"So, if this story is true, he convinced the other Tulureans she was a witch?" I asked.

That sounded far too much like my story with Dante.

"That's what the story claims. My great-grandmother's journal says the shapeshifter blood made Shadow Walkers better trackers," he explained.

"Great," I muttered. "So, if this story is true, then your shapeshifter genes made you a better killer."

He shrugged. "I suppose that's one way of looking at it."

"I'm still not buying any of this," I told him. "Why did your great-grandmother keep a journal with this story if it was supposed to be some big secret?"

"She was a hopeless romantic," he explained. "There are also rumors that she may have advocated for better treatment of familiars, but my father says that's just a lie spread by families who don't like the Shadow Walkers."

"I find it hard to believe a shapeshifter could have pretended to be a witch for very long," I told him. "It was hard keeping my identity a secret for even a short time, and if this story is true, she was here long enough to have five children. Someone must have been suspicious."

"I'm sure they were, but when she gave birth to strong, healthy spellcaster children who became leaders in the Shadow Walker family, they probably stopped worrying. Her children were all spellcasters, so why would anyone be suspicious after that?"

"That makes sense, though I have a hard time believing a shapeshifter could be happy with her children becoming hunters and killers."

"We all do what we have to in order to survive," he argued.

"By sacrificing others," I stated. "That's not the legacy I hope to leave behind. Let's skip forward to the part about you claiming my mother was a Shadow Walker."

"Eliza," he whispered. "It was her sixteenth birthday, and she'd gone out to hunt with me that day. Thankfully, it was just the two of us. This could have ended much differently had my father been with us. She started to feel off, so we stopped to rest. Before my very eyes, she turned into a black cat."

"Was this before or after you'd read the stories?"

"Before," he replied. "I panicked at first. I saw her struggling to free herself from her clothing, so I pulled it together and helped her. When I looked into her eyes, I knew it was my sister, but I didn't know what to do for her. I messed up and told my father about what had happened."

"I take it he reacted poorly and ordered her banished."

He took a deep breath before admitting, "He ordered me to kill her."

"His own daughter?"

I don't know why that surprised me.

He nodded. "He believes I killed her. Instead, I arranged a meeting with your father and begged him to let Eliza stay at the Heathergate Refuge. It wasn't easy keeping her hidden until your father agreed to take her in. By then, I could tell there was something between them. The last time I saw her, she was with him and a female shapeshifter named Fiona."

I said nothing as his words sank in.

I wanted to continue arguing that he was mistaken or insist he was making this up for some reason.

Deep down, I knew it was true, and it explained a lot. I shouldn't have been able to channel Dante's magic. I shouldn't have been able to bond with him. These things could be explained by me having spellcaster blood.

It was true.

"I really am Juliet Shadow Walker," I whispered.

He smiled, seeming relieved that I'd stopped arguing. "Yes, you are. When Nicolas Verdugo came here asking about Juliet Shadow Walker, my father told him there wasn't anyone in our family by that name. Since he thinks your mother is long dead, he had no reason to make the connection."

"But you knew she hadn't died. How did you find me?"

"Nicolas asked for my help hunting you because I'm an excellent tracker," he explained. "That's how I found you."

I felt numb as Kaine watched me.

"You look so much like your mother," he began. "It's like I'm staring at Eliza."

"Except I'm not Eliza," I stated. "Why did you bring me here? Your father will want me dead if he finds out what I am, and I'm sure he's not the only one."

"I'll figure out a way to keep you safe," he promised. "You're my niece, and I'm not going to let anyone hurt you. Others know who you are and will also protect you."

That was more than I'd had in Azuredale, but I was still surrounded by enemies. My experience had taught me that this would not end well, especially when Nicolas was still in the picture. None of that mattered. I couldn't stay, even if Kaine made it safe for me.

"I have to get back to Dante and the others," I told him.

"Why?" he asked. "They're safe from the Azureans at the Heathergate Refuge."

"Safe from the Azureans, but not safe," I argued. "It will help them some that two of my father's trusted guards know they were helping me, but I just left two spellcasters, a rogue shapeshifter, and a demon to try to explain what happened to me."

"A demon?" he asked.

"The female with the red eyes," I explained.

He nodded. "She's the only reason we were able to get you away from there. She really helped us in the fight."

"Where is she now?" I asked.

He shrugged. "I don't know. It's possible she entered the Heathergate Refuge after the fight. My goal was to get you to safety, not worry about strange females."

So, they had no clue where Sin was or if she was okay. Then a thought occurred to me.

"Did you see a dog after the fight?"

He nodded. "Yes, Calista carried her to the car. She seemed quite upset by the fighting. I've got her at my place. Is she yours?"

"Yes, can you bring her to me?"

"All right," he agreed. "I'll bring her by later. In the meantime, you should eat more and rest. That spell Nicolas hit you with could have killed you. You're very lucky to be alive."

He started to leave before looking at me over his shoulder. "I really do just want to protect you, Juliet."

"Thank you for saving me."

"I'd give my life for you," he assured me. "You're my niece."

"But you wouldn't save any other shapeshifter," I whispered after the door closed behind him.

Chapter Four

Calista brought Sin to me later that day, explaining that Kaine had gotten busy with work.

Once I was alone in the room with Sin, who'd immediately sprawled out on my bed, I asked, "Could you change to your human form so we can talk? I have a lot of questions."

Sin didn't change right away, instead sitting up and regarding me with one raised ear.

"I need to talk to you about Dante and the others," I explained. "We have to find a way to help them."

Sin changed into her human form. Instead of her usual flowing dress, she wore black pants, a red short-sleeve shirt, and black ankle boots. "Why must I always rescue all of you? Can't you take care of yourselves for even a second?"

"I'm sorry you keep having to rescue us," I replied. "I appreciate your help. We all do."

She waved off my words. "I suppose saving you is more entertaining than anything I've done in the last century or so. I miss Dante. He's my favorite."

"I miss him, too," I said with a sad sigh.

"Have you tried your telepathic link?" she asked.

I frowned. "No, I haven't. That should have been the

first thing I did."

"It won't work, anyway," she told me.

"How do you know?" I asked.

"That spell around the Heathergate Refuge is locked up tight. It's going to block all magic from getting past the barrier," she explained.

I'm stubborn, so I tried, but she was right. I could follow the threads of mine and Dante's joined magic only so far before being met with a metaphysical brick wall.

"You just tried it, didn't you?"

"Did you think I wouldn't?" I asked her.

"No, I was honestly surprised you hadn't tried before," she admitted. "I like the idea of going after Dante and Serena, but I'm not sure how we're going to get to them. I felt it when the spell around the Heathergate Refuge started to close."

"Close?" I asked.

She nodded. "It stopped letting anyone in or out. I felt it happening. That's why I tried rushing everyone across. I decided to send you across last, but I didn't get the chance."

"So, you like me even less than Geori?"

"Someone is feeling a little paranoid," she mused. "I didn't like the idea of being stuck on this side with him. You're not too bad. I was also closer to the others, so I pushed them first."

"Do you have any idea why the spell closed the barrier?" I asked.

"Oh, I know why," she said, her lips pressed together in a thin line.

"Peony betrayed us," I said with a sigh. "There's something in the bracelets she gave us that altered the protection spell."

"That would be my guess," she agreed. "It's always possible someone else meddled with the spell on the bracelets before she gave them to you, but I don't think anyone else could have managed something quite this powerful. It's probably temporary, but at least for now, no one can get in or out of the Heathergate Refuge."

I felt tears burn the backs of my eyes, but I fought them. Now wasn't the time to feel sorry for myself.

Yes, I was frustrated, angry, and sad, but I needed to come up with a plan, not wallow in self-pity.

"It's kind of crazy that this is the second time you've been unable to contact Dante telepathically because of magic blocking you," she remarked.

That gave me an idea.

"Dante said you were able to help us share a dream before," I began. "Do you think you could do that again?"

She tapped her chin as she considered my question. "I might be able to do that. It worked last time because my magic was involved with the protection spell preventing Dante from contacting you. That made it easier to work around the spell. I'm not completely sure what magic was used this time, but I'm willing to try."

"When?" I asked.

She shrugged. "It will only work when you're both asleep, so tonight would be best."

I looked at the brightly lit sky outside my room and sighed. "I hate waiting."

She smiled, revealing a hint of her tiny fangs. "Me too, but I'm not close enough to force Dante to go to sleep. Is that the only plan you have so far? Wait until Dante might be asleep and try to share a dream?"

"No, I think we should try to go to the facility where the spellcasters dispose of the dead shapeshifters."

"That's more morbid than I would have expected from you," she remarked. "Why would we go there? You don't want to try reanimating any corpses, do you? That never works out well."

"Reanimate corpses?" I asked. "Why would I want to do that?"

She rolled her eyes. "To create an undead army, of course."

"Is that even possible?" I asked.

"No, reanimated corpses are terrible at following

orders," she explained. "Why do you want to go there?"

"Do you remember the warlock we met when we got the bracelets?" I asked. "Erik."

She nodded. "The pretty one."

"I want to talk to him since he may have some ideas about what was done to our bracelets. I'd also like to get word to another spellcaster in Azuredale. That warlock may have some idea of how we can get past the Ivorfalls since his family makes the bracelets for the Heathergate Refuge."

She frowned. "To recap: spellcasters want you dead, so you'd like to meet up with more of them?"

"Three," I replied. "I think Dante's brother, Ambrose, may be able to help us contact Erik and Torrent."

"I suppose I can always kill them if they're a problem," she mused. "Where are we?"

"We're in a spellcaster prison."

"It doesn't look like a prison," she pointed out.

"It is, and I'm not convinced Kaine will let me leave. I'm not locked in, but if he prevents me from leaving, I'm a prisoner."

"Why did he bring you here?" she asked. "I was surprised when he fought so hard to keep you alive. I don't think I'd have been able to save you without the help of the Shadow Walkers."

"He claims to be my uncle," I replied.

"Now, it makes sense!"

"What makes sense?" I asked. "As near as I can tell, none of this makes any sense."

"I kept thinking that either Dante had to be part-shapeshifter or you had to be part-spellcaster. Now, I know it's you that has the mixed blood."

"I'm still having a hard time believing that."

She laughed and waved off my denial. "Liar."

"Okay, it explains a lot, and I believe it. I just don't like it."

"You should see if your new family can help you," she suggested.

I shook my head. "I don't trust them."

She shrugged. "So, what are we going to do now?"

"Figure out a good time to leave," I replied. "It would help if you keep pretending to be a dog around the Shadow Walkers. I'm not sure what they'll do if they know I have a demon helping me."

"Fine with me," she agreed. "Kaine gives a great belly rub. Are you sure you don't want to bring your uncle with us? He tastes good."

I frowned. "You want to eat my uncle?"

"Just lick him," she replied as if I was crazy for thinking otherwise. "I'm bored with all this talking, so I'm going to change back to a dog. Will you rub my belly?"

"Okay," I replied.

Chapter Five

Kaine didn't return to my room that day.

Calista dropped off food and rubbed Sin's belly before declaring that Sin was the most beautiful dog she'd ever seen. She didn't stay to talk, insisting she had work to get done.

I was bored out of my mind most of the day and had trouble falling asleep that night. I tossed and turned as Sin watched me from the end of my mattress.

When the door opened, I quickly sat up in bed, my heart pounding against my ribs.

"Dante?" I asked in a ragged voice as he slipped into the room.

His long brown hair was tied back, and his silvery-blue eyes held confusion as he scanned my room. The stubble that had been on his chin the last time I'd seen him was gone.

"Where are we?"

I let out a sad sigh. "You aren't here, are you?"

"No, I can't be here," he replied. "We're trapped on opposite sides of a spell. This has to be a dream."

"A dream," I mused. "I must have dozed off, and Sin connected our dreams."

When I stood, he moved closer and tried to wrap me in

his arms, but they went right through me.

"It's so annoying that I can't touch you. Do you think Sin does this on purpose? I couldn't touch you in the other dream we shared either."

I shrugged. "It's hard to say. I'm glad she was able to help me see you, even if it is just in a dream."

"I'm so glad you're okay," he murmured. "I've been going crazy trying to get to you. The spell closed around us, and I can't figure out what happened. It may have been Sin, though I've been wracking my brain to figure out why she'd do this."

"It wasn't Sin," I told him. "We think it was Peony."

"So the demon betrayed us," he remarked. "Why do you suppose she would do something like this?"

"I'm not sure," I replied. "Sin doesn't know either."

"I'm glad Sin stayed with you," he stated. "Where are you?"

"The Tulurgate Peninsula."

"Juliet Shadow Walker," he whispered. "I can't believe my lie turned out to be the truth."

"Who told you about me being a Shadow Walker?" I asked.

"Fiona," he replied. "She said your mother was Eliza Shadow Walker."

"That's what I've been told," I replied. "Kaine Shadow Walker claims to be my uncle. He and two other Shadow Walkers saved me."

"Do they accept you there?" Dante asked.

"Only a few know I'm here. If the wrong Shadow Walkers figure out I'm hiding in their prison, this won't end well for me."

"Prison? Why are you in prison if Kaine accepts you?"

"I don't know why they're hiding me here, but I'm not locked up," I explained. "Calista even showed me the way out."

He looked around. "This doesn't look like a prison cell. Are you sure this is their prison?"

"You saw the corridor."

He shook his head. "I was already walking into this room when I entered the dream. I'm annoyed that Kaine put you in prison."

"Like I said, I'm at the prison, but not in prison," I reminded him. "That's what Kaine claims, at least. I just don't know. I'm pretty sure I could walk out of this building, but it's not safe out there."

"It sounds like a prison," he grumbled. "I'm so tired of being separated from you. How are we going to get back to each other? I walked the perimeter of the spell until I was too exhausted to take another step, and I plan to walk more tomorrow, but I'm not sure I'll find a weakness in the spell."

"Sin believes it will weaken with time, but she's not completely sure," I told him. "She wasn't sure she could make the shared dream happen."

"I'm glad she did," he replied. "I'm still worried about you being surrounded by Tulureans, but it's better than the constant worry that you were dead or that Nicolas had you."

"This seems better than being captured by Azureans, at least for now. I'm hoping to leave with Sin soon."

"Are you coming back to the Heathergate Refuge to try to get past the spell?"

"Yes, but only after I talk to Erik and Torrent," I replied.

"No," he said with a shake of his head. "There's no way for you to safely talk to either of them. The only places you could find Erik is at Peony's settlement or the disposal center. You have enemies at both places. Erik may be one of them. Torrent is at Azuredale, and going there would be a suicide mission."

"I need you to trust me, Dante," I began. "Sin will be with me. I think the only way I can get to the Heathergate Refuge is with Torrent or Erik's help. Even if the spell disruption ends up being temporary, we have no way of knowing how long it will last."

"Would it help to know that Darius has already

sounded the warning on your stepmother? I don't know what's going on there, but Fiona sent him back with instructions to only talk to certain people and to tell your father about the Shadow Walkers recognizing you."

"I can't believe my father kept this from me," I muttered.

"I can," Dante replied. "This would have made you an outcast among your people, and you couldn't have had any kind of relationship with the Shadow Walkers. What good would it have done to tell you?"

"I don't know, but I'm still not happy that he kept it from me. I guess I understand why he might have thought it was for the best. Maybe he planned to tell me when I was older."

"You'll have a chance to ask him," Dante assured me. "We have to figure this spell out."

"I need something from you," I began. "This will help me on my end."

"What do you need?"

"Ambrose's hunting schedule," I told him.

"Why?" he asked.

"I think he's my best bet for getting to Torrent and Erik," I explained.

"He might help," Dante hesitantly agreed. "I can't guarantee it, but I don't think he'll sound the alarm on you if he refuses to help. The problem is, I don't know his schedule."

"I thought you said the rotation doesn't change."

"It doesn't," he agreed. "It's just that Ambrose isn't on the regular rotation. He fills in when someone is off. The only way I'd know where he's going to be is if I know about someone being off long-term."

"Like if someone disappeared?" I asked.

"Yes, Ambrose would likely be assigned their work," he replied.

"Nicolas is in a cell down the hall from me," I explained. "I don't think Kaine told your family he has him locked up, but either way, Nicolas's spot will need to be filled for the foreseeable future."

"All right," he agreed. "I can give you Nicolas's schedule, but be careful. It's always possible someone else was assigned to his rotation. Ambrose may be covering my old hunting territory, though I think they've likely divided it up by now."

"I'll be careful," I promised him. "Who do you think is more likely to help me, Erik or Torrent?"

He hesitated. "I trust Torrent more than Erik, but I don't know who can best help you. I'm inclined to think it's Erik because he has a connection with Peony."

"I'll talk it over with Sin tomorrow and see what she thinks."

"I love—"

He was suddenly ripped from our dream. The loss of his presence was so jarring that I jerked awake.

"No!"

Sin sat beside the bed, watching me. "Did it work?"

"It worked," I told her with a shaky smile. "I guess he was suddenly awoken. At least, I hope that's the case."

"That's probably it," she agreed. "Don't start obsessing over how Dante left the dream. Sometimes, even if people wake up slowly, they suddenly leave a dream."

I nodded. "I'll try to stop worrying."

"So, what did he say?" she asked.

I gave her a brief rundown of the highlights of our conversation. I'd noticed that Sin did best when there weren't many details to bore her.

"So, we need to decide who to ask first," I told her.

"Silly shapeshifter," she said under her breath. "Dante's brother will be the first person we contact since we need his help either way. We can ask who he thinks we should talk to first. Do you think we can trust him?"

"I don't know," I admitted. "My gut tells me he won't betray me."

"Then we'll have to go with that," she replied before clapping. "This is such a fun adventure."

"Being in a Tulurean prison?" I asked. "Or is it the part

about finding Ambrose?"

"Everything since I decided to follow Dante," she explained. "This is the most fun I've had in centuries! I hope we keep having fun adventures."

"I'd like a break from adventures," I told her.

"Are we leaving now?" she asked.

"Not yet," I replied. "Dante got pulled from the dream before I could get Nicolas's hunting schedule. He thinks Ambrose will be handling his rotation."

She waved off my concerns. "That's not a problem. Nicolas is right down the hall. We can convince him to share his hunting schedule with us."

"I don't trust him," I told her. "I'd be willing to bet any schedule he gives us is a lie that will land us in the path of hunters like his father."

"Yes, it would make sense for him to do something like that," she agreed. "He's an interesting warlock as well— smart and ruthless."

"Sadistic and evil," I argued.

She shrugged. "Also true, but he'd make a terrible companion, so it doesn't matter how many fine qualities he has. I'll try connecting your dream to Dante's again tomorrow. This time, don't get distracted. Get the schedule and then chat."

"All right," I agreed. "I wish I'd had more time with him tonight. I don't want to wait around a second longer."

"Not even to get to know your family?" she asked.

"They aren't my family," I insisted. "We may share blood, but they kill my kind. I'm thankful some of them helped me, but I'll be happy if I never see them again."

Chapter Six

I was glad to be out of my room, but not sure I liked the idea of spending the day with Kaine and Calista. Aside from not being sure I wanted to get to know either of them better, I was still worried someone would realize I didn't belong there, or worse, recognize me from Azuredale despite our efforts to mask my identity.

"Stop looking so nervous," Kaine told me when he pulled me aside near their market area. "You keep looking around as if someone might attack you. Everyone here sees a young Shadow Walker who hasn't started training yet."

Had I been a Tulurean, I'd have already started hunting by my seventeenth birthday, so Kaine had used a cloaking spell to make me look younger. He claimed that it would be easy to pass me off as an eleven-year-old witch with my size. My mother had been small, but he didn't think anyone would make that connection since they'd all heard shapeshifters had killed her.

"What if your father sees me?" I whispered. "Won't he notice that I look like my mother and have questions?"

Kaine shook his head. "He'll assume you're the daughter of my mistress. That's assuming he sees you. My father doesn't go to the market area all that often."

"He's not quite right in the head," Calista added. "I'm

not sure he should still be hunting."

Kaine glared at her. "Show some respect for the head of our family. My father is still a great leader."

His defense of the man who'd ordered my mother's death was further proof we couldn't be a happy family.

"He's the one Nicolas talked to about me, right?"

Kaine nodded. "Yes."

I said nothing more as he started walking again.

The market area on the Tulurgate Peninsula was quite different from the one in Azuredale. Rather than large buildings, portable stalls were set up. Some Tulureans were cooking food outside at their booths, while others sold jewelry, clothing, or weapons.

The whole community was quite different from Azuredale, and I could see why it had been easy to explain my surprise at how the Azureans lived. Rather than large estates, the Tulureans lived in smaller homes. They often walked places, though they had vehicles for longer trips around the peninsula as well as for when they needed to leave the area.

Sin didn't stand out since there were dogs of all sizes. Some Tulureans even carried small dogs around in special bags.

I stopped at a stall selling knives when one caught my eye.

"This is beautiful," I said in awe as I looked at the ornate carvings on the metal hilt.

The witch running the stall grinned. "I think it's my best work."

I looked at the other blades on the table. "It is, though the others are also beautiful. Can I hold it?"

The witch looked over my shoulder at Kaine for his permission, and I almost said something before remembering I was in the guise of a child.

"She's quite good with a blade," Kaine assured the witch.

The witch handed me the knife, and I felt a soft hum of energy flowing through it.

"What is this spell?" I asked.

"You feel the spell?" she asked in surprise.

"Yes," I replied as I continued to look down at the knife, which felt so natural in my hand. The weight and size were perfect, as if it had been custom made for me. "It's not strong, but I feel something."

"Interesting," she mused. "It seems you're meant to have this blade."

I'd have accused her of using some sales pitch on me if I didn't feel the same about the knife. I didn't want to put it down.

"We'll take it," Kaine announced, much to my surprise.

After we left that table, Kaine took me to be fitted for a sheath for the knife. The warlock selling the sheath argued that I should get something bigger that I could grow into, but Kaine insisted I'd never leave such a beautiful knife sitting in a drawer until I grew into the sheath.

I still wasn't crazy about Kaine, but I appreciated his generosity. The blade would be helpful when I left the Tulurgate Peninsula.

"Orlando is trying to get our attention," Calista told Kaine after I put the knife in the new sheath.

Kaine sighed before looking at me. "Stay here while we see what he wants."

"Can I continue looking at the stalls?" I asked. "It will look funny if I just stand here."

He nodded. "All right. Don't go too far."

I started walking by the stands selling clothing. Nothing caught my eye, so I moved on to the ones selling boots. I still had my Azurean boots, so I didn't need any, but I was curious to see if the Tulureans had anything of that quality.

"Try these," a witch who was shopping suggested when she saw me looking at a pair of brown ankle boots.

The boots she'd gestured to would go over my knees. "Are they easy to move in?"

She pointed to her matching boots. "They're very comfortable in the colder months."

The warlock selling the boots chimed in. "These are my best seller this time of year. Would you like to try a pair?"

I shook my head. "No, I don't think I'd like wearing something that high up."

I also didn't want to have a second pair of boots to carry.

When I turned, I came face to face with a warlock who looked like an older version of Kaine.

"Eliza?" His voice was raw as he said my mother's name, and I felt panic grip me.

Kaine had seemed certain no one would notice my strong resemblance to my mother since she'd been gone for nearly twenty years. All but a few Tulureans thought she was dead. The spell also made me look much younger than she had the last time any Tulurean had seen her.

I shook my head. "No, I'm not Eliza."

He stared at me in an unnerving manner.

"Father!" Kaine called out as he hurried toward us. "I thought you were hunting today."

The warlock didn't look away from me as he responded to Kaine. "The day was a waste, so I decided to come back early. I wanted to get a new tunic for your mother. She's been in a mood lately, and I thought it would cheer her up."

"That's a great idea," Kaine agreed. "I'm sure she'll appreciate that."

"Who is this? She looks exactly like Eliza."

Kaine pretended to study me before shaking his head. "I can see the resemblance, but she's only eleven, so I'm sure she'll be taller than Eliza. I suppose they have similar features."

His father nodded. "Yes, she is young. Who is she, and why haven't I met her before?"

"You don't want me to bring any of my children around," Kaine reminded him.

"I'd like it if you found an acceptable witch to bond with and brought your children with her around," he snapped. "We have methods of preventing pregnancy. Try using some of them with your mistresses."

Kaine's eyes flashed with anger. "Sorry, I haven't found a witch that can live up to your standards yet. Now, if you'll excuse me, I need to get my daughter home to her mother."

He caught my arm to draw me away.

"Bring her by for dinner tonight," his father ordered.

"Her mother?" Kaine asked.

His father's eyes flashed with anger. "Don't play games. I'm in a bad mood today. Bring your daughter. Her mother can come, as well." He looked at me. "What's your name?"

My name?

Why hadn't we come up with a name for me to give others while we were out?

This was sloppy. Since Nicolas had already asked about me, we couldn't use my real name, but no names came to me.

"Ella," Kaine replied. "I'm not sure it's such a good idea to bring her to your home. You know how that will look."

His father let out a tired sigh. "I'm getting tired of caring about how things will look. Bring her tonight."

He walked away, not waiting for further argument.

"Ella?" Calista whispered when we were away from the market area. She continued when Kaine nodded. "You're using the nickname you gave your sister?"

Kaine shrugged. "Why not? Only a few people know I called her that. I doubt my parents remember, but if they do, it won't seem suspicious."

"I can't go to dinner at his house," I argued. "Can you make up an excuse?"

"Not unless you want him to go looking for you," Kaine replied. "Don't worry. I'll prepare you for all you'll need to know. He'll probably be bored with the idea by the time we get there and ignore you the whole evening. Even if he doesn't, he'll talk around you. Trust me. My father does not

interact with children."
"Let's hope you're right."

Chapter Seven

After our run-in with his father, Kaine spent the next couple of hours preparing me for dinner at my grandfather's place.

That's how I ended up at the home of a witch who looked like she wasn't the least bit happy about a visit from Kaine. She stood in the doorway with her arms crossed in front of her chest.

The witch was beautiful, with dark red hair that went just past her ears, a curvy frame, soft blue eyes, and ivory skin that looked almost too perfect to be real. She wasn't much taller than me.

I'd been told she'd help us with my cover story, but it didn't look like she'd be willing to help Kaine with anything.

"Why are you here?" she demanded.

"Ah, so you're still mad," Kaine remarked with a grin.

"Mad?" she asked. "Why would I be mad? Just because you think I'm not good enough for you?"

Kaine let out a sigh. "I never said that."

"But you didn't defend me against those accusations," she shot back.

"Can we come inside?" he asked. "Please, Faye. I know you're angry with me, and I don't blame you, but I need your help. You're the only one I can trust."

She hesitated only a heartbeat before nodding and stepping back so we could enter.

"What do you want, Kaine?" she asked.

He looked at her with such longing that I knew he cared deeply for her. "I want so many things."

She snorted. "I know you didn't bring a child with you to try sweet-talking me."

"No, I didn't," he agreed. "I need you to pretend to be this girl's mother."

"Why would I do that?" she asked. "Who is her mother?"

"Eliza," he replied. "This is my niece, Juliet, and she's going to end up dead like my sister if we don't help her."

Faye looked at me with wide eyes. "How is this possible?"

"Can we sit down?" Kaine asked. "This is a long story."

Faye nodded, and we all went into her small sitting area, where Kaine told her what was going on.

"Why would you take her to the market where anyone could see her?" Faye demanded.

"I wondered the same thing," I replied.

She smiled at me. "Because you clearly got your mother's brains."

"I didn't think my father would be in the area, and I figured that even if he was, he'd never look twice at a child," he insisted.

"You should have been more prepared," she told him. "Your father has gotten stranger each year. Why do you think he'll believe Juliet is my child?"

"Because he doesn't know anything about any of the other witches I've been involved with," he explained.

"How many witches are you seeing?" I asked.

"None right now," he replied. "I don't have any children, either, despite what my father thinks. There have been rumors, and my father believed them. I never did anything to disprove them."

"Because Kaine has daddy issues," Faye replied.

"Faye," he warned. "We don't have time to fight."

"Why do you think she'll help you when there's obviously a lot of resentment between the two of you?" I asked.

"He's counting on me wanting to help you, and he figures I'll be able to pull off the lie because I avoid everyone," Faye explained. "There are few Tulureans who would know with certainty that I don't have a child."

"Faye has lived the life of a hermit for more than a decade," Kaine explained.

She looked even more irritated. "Not many people wanted to be around me after your father made such a point of dragging my name through the mud. With no one defending me, they believed every word he said."

Kaine let out a tired sigh. "Can we not do this in front of Juliet? She already doesn't think very highly of me."

"You hunt my kind," I reminded him.

"You were able to forgive Dante Verdugo," he pointed out.

Faye glared at him. "Stop acting like a petulant child, Kaine. I love you, and even I have trouble accepting what you do."

"Are you going to help me?" Kaine asked.

Faye rolled her eyes. "Not in this lifetime. I'm going to help Juliet because I don't want her getting killed by your ignorant family."

"I need you to have dinner at my father's house to help me pull this off," Kaine told her.

"No!" she practically shouted. "There's no way am I going near any Shadow Walker home. You had better come up with another plan."

Chapter Eight

"I can't believe he talked me into this," Faye muttered as we approached my grandfather's home.

It felt strange thinking of him as my grandfather.

Kaine had wanted me to return to his home after visiting Faye, but Faye had convinced him that it would look less suspicious this way. Kaine didn't have any children living with him, something my grandfather knew.

I was glad to be away from my uncle and the other Shadow Walkers for a few hours before we needed to go for dinner. Staying at Faye's home was also helpful since it meant I wouldn't have to walk out of the prison or Kaine's house when I left the Tulurgate Peninsula. Faye also lived on the outskirts of the community.

"Thank you for doing this for me," I told her.

She flashed me a smile. "Kaine always has had a way of talking me into doing things I shouldn't."

"Love can make us do crazy things," I replied, thinking of all Dante had done for me.

"Sadly, we don't always love the right person," she said with a sad smile.

"How long were you together?" I asked. "If I'm not being too nosy."

"It's fine," she assured me. "We were together off and

on for about ten years—until I got tired of being his dirty secret. I've had some slips, like when he was seriously injured a couple of years ago. It's always a mistake giving him another chance."

"Is that what you're doing now?" I asked.

She shook her head. "No, I'm definitely not giving him another chance. If you want to repay me for helping you, remind me of that if it looks like I'm wavering."

My grandfather lived in a small house not far from the market area. I learned on the way there that most Shadow Walkers lived in that area. Kaine's home was farther away, along with Calista's, but Faye didn't know why they lived away from the others.

We were greeted at the door by a witch with dark skin, long black hair, and golden-brown eyes.

"Oh my," she whispered as she stared at me. "When I heard about you and how much you resemble my Eliza, I didn't believe it. I thought my warlock was exaggerating, but you could be Eliza's twin."

I didn't know what to say or how to react. This woman looked like she was about to burst into tears.

Did she know my mother had changed into a cat?

Had she heard about her warlock ordering my mother's death?

"This is my daughter, Ella," Faye told her.

My grandmother cleared her throat, and I watched as she composed herself. It was an amazing transformation from grieving mother to distant hostess.

"It's nice to meet you, Ella." Her tone no longer held any warmth. "I'm surprised Kaine never mentioned having a child with you, Faye."

"Why would he?" Faye asked. "He was told to stay away from me and to never bring me anywhere near this family again. Why would he want to admit to having a child with me?"

My grandmother sighed and nodded. "Yes, I can see why you didn't bring Ella here before. I'm surprised you agreed to come today."

"Kaine asked me," Faye explained.

"So, you're still seeing each other?" my grandmother asked as we followed her into the dining room.

Faye let out a bark of laughter. "No, we are definitely no longer seeing each other."

My grandmother stopped walking and looked around before hugging Faye.

Faye looked shocked and remained stiff in her embrace.

"I always liked you," my grandmother whispered. "Kaine loved you so much. I think he still loves you."

"No, he doesn't," Faye replied as she stepped away from my grandmother. "I know you're trying to be nice, but you don't have to. Your warlock hates me and considers me a mistake from your son's past. I've moved on."

My grandmother hesitated before nodding and looking at me. "You're so quiet, Ella."

"I'm not sure what to say," I admitted. "This has been a strange day."

"Yes, it has," my grandmother agreed. "Have a seat, and I'll see if I can find our missing warlocks. We should eat before the food gets cold."

After she left the room, I sat beside Faye.

"This is more uncomfortable than I thought it would be," I remarked.

"Oh, it's going to get worse," she stated. "You can get away with not talking much because of your age. They'll focus more on me."

She'd told me that several times as she'd prepared me for our dinner with the Shadow Walker family.

She looked around before leaning in and whispering, "You're welcome to stay with me as long as you like."

"Why are you doing this for me?" I asked. "I know what you said earlier, but I still feel like this is a lot, considering how strained things are between you and Kaine. I need to stop calling him that."

She waved off my concern. "Don't worry about that. This family isn't big on familial titles. You could alternate what you call him in the same sentence, and no one would think it's odd."

I didn't respond because I heard angry voices approaching.

"Why do you care so much about me bringing her here?" Kaine demanded. "You're the one who always told me that only children from a witch I'm bound to matter to you."

"You didn't think that one who looks exactly like your sister would be an exception?" my grandfather snapped. "Are there others who look like Eliza?"

"Both of you stop arguing," my grandmother told them. "You're going to scare that poor child. She won't want to come back here."

"That's something we have in common," Kaine said under his breath before pasting a smile on his face and approaching us. "Thank you for bringing Ella tonight, Faye. After the way my family treated you, I wouldn't have blamed you for refusing to join us."

"And then they would have been at my place demanding to see Ella," she reminded him. "None of you care all that much about what I want."

"I'm sorry," Kaine said softly. "Really, Faye, I am sorry."

"Sorry for what?" my grandfather demanded.

"Everything," Kaine replied before sitting on my other side.

"I made all of Eliza's favorites," my grandmother announced, leading to several awkward beats of silence.

"Interesting choice," Kaine replied with a tight smile.

My grandparents both excused themselves to grab the food from the kitchen, and the silence continued until they returned with several trays of meat and bread, all smothered in strong-smelling sauces.

It seemed I hadn't inherited my mother's taste in food. The sauces were all too strong, and I had to force myself to swallow each bite.

My grandmother spent the meal talking about her lost

daughter, not giving anyone a chance to add much to the conversation.

My grandfather just stared at me.

I'd never had a more strained meal in my life, and that said a lot, considering the tension at some meals with my stepmother.

Though I'd been told I wouldn't have to talk much at the meal, I'd had my doubts. As it turned out, other than questions about how I liked the food, no one asked me anything.

"Eliza was a very powerful witch," my grandmother said for perhaps the tenth time. "Is Ella also powerful?" she asked Faye.

"Yes, but not in any skills that would help with hunting," Faye replied. "She takes after my side."

"That's a shame," my grandfather replied.

"Why is that?" Kaine asked as he studied his father.

My grandfather let out a tired sigh. "Listen, Kaine, I know I've made a lot of mistakes." His gaze shifted to me. "When I saw you, Ella, it was at a time when I was dwelling on those mistakes and the demons that haunt me."

"All we can do is learn from our mistakes and try to do better in the future," I replied.

My grandfather stared at me for several heartbeats before replying. "You are very wise for someone so young." He cleared his throat and looked at Kaine. "I think you should take Faye as your witch."

"You what?" Kaine practically shouted.

"I'd like to have Ella be a full member of this family, and accepting Faye is the only way to make that happen," he explained with a casual shrug.

My grandmother smiled and covered her mouth as Faye stood and said, "I think it's time I took Ella home."

"Why?" My grandfather looked genuinely baffled by her response. "You've always wanted to elevate your status by joining this family, and I'm now giving you that opportunity."

"No," Faye replied in a clipped tone. "I loved Kaine. I

still love Kaine, but I'm not about to join your family."

"Kaine," my grandfather began, "change her mind."

"Yes, Kaine," my grandmother said happily. "This is for the best."

"It's not going to happen," Faye insisted.

"I should probably walk Faye and Ella home," Kaine announced as he stood.

"First, I have another matter I need to discuss with you," my grandfather began.

"What's that?" Kaine asked.

"Why is Nicolas Verdugo being held in our prison? His father isn't happy."

"Nicolas Verdugo is here?" Faye sounded uneasy.

How many women had he terrorized?

"When did you hear about that?" Kaine asked.

"I saw him at the prison shortly before you arrived here for dinner," my grandfather replied. "There wasn't time to bring it up before you started making demands regarding my behavior with Faye tonight."

I saw the tension Kaine tried to hide. "What did Nicolas tell you?"

"That you helped his familiar and his fugitive brother escape," my grandfather replied, his gaze locked on Kaine.

Faye's laughter drew everyone's attention. "Sorry," she said with a hand over her mouth as she pretended to try to get her laughter under control. "Nicolas Verdugo is claiming to have a familiar?"

"I thought the Azureans didn't allow hunters to have familiars," I remarked.

"They don't," Faye stated. "They follow the same rules as the Shadow Walkers when it comes to familiars. Why is he really locked up?"

"He tried killing Calista," Kaine replied. "Nicolas claimed to have a lead on that shapeshifter who was pretending to be a Shadow Walker." He looked at his father. "Jenna, was it?"

My grandfather shrugged. "I don't recall. Why didn't you tell me about this?"

"It didn't seem important," Kaine replied. "Besides, you were busy with other matters. I probably should have refused to help the Verdugos, but I was curious and bored. When I caught up with Nicolas, he was trying to prevent a group of shapeshifters with bracelets from entering the Heathergate Refuge. One of the shapeshifters claimed to be the daughter of the leader. Once they crossed the Ivorfalls, proving they belonged there, Nicolas went crazy and said he'd wait there for them to come out again. After Calista suggested he leave, he attacked her. He hasn't made much more sense since we got him back here."

My grandfather nodded. "Nicolas was never quite right in the head. I don't know why his father trusts him so much. I'm still not sure we should be this involved. Does anyone on the council know we have him locked up?"

"No," Kaine admitted. "I don't plan to keep him here forever, just until he's recovered from his injuries."

My grandfather nodded. "Yes, it's best if we don't send him back too banged up. How long does the healer think he'll need to recover?"

"Another week," Kaine replied.

"All right," my grandfather agreed. "I'll try to find a way to explain this to his father. I'd rather not have any trouble with the rest of the Verdugos."

"I think we've all traumatized Ella enough for one day," Kaine stated. "I'm going to walk her and Faye home."

Once we were farther from the clusters of homes and nearing Faye's house, she stopped and jabbed Kaine's chest with her index finger. "Why is Nicolas Verdugo here?"

"Because he tried to kill Juliet," Kaine replied with a shrug.

"And you kept him alive?" she demanded.

"I've been wondering why you did that as well," I added. "Nicolas is going to try to kill me again. He's also your enemy now."

"I can't kill him," Kaine argued.

"Someone needs to," I replied.

"Exactly," Faye agreed. "We'll walk the rest of the way

without you."

"Fine," Kaine bit out. "I'll be by tomorrow, but it probably won't be until the afternoon."

He looked like he was going to say more, but in

Chapter Nine

Neither of us said much as we walked the rest of the way back to Faye's place.

Once we were at her door, I said, "I'm so glad you're letting me stay with you. Do you think it's possible I'm not related to the Shadow Walkers?"

She laughed as she opened the door. "I don't blame you for hoping, but you are a Shadow Walker."

She jumped back and put an arm out as if to stop me when she opened the door.

"Who are you?" Faye demanded as I felt her gathering her magic for a fight.

"What are you doing, Sin?" I asked when I saw her standing by the window in human form.

"Waiting for you to get back," Sin replied as if it was obvious.

"I thought you were going to stay in dog form so none of the Tulureans would know what you are."

"She's a shapeshifter?" Faye asked.

"Ew, no!" Sin sounded offended.

"What's wrong with being a shapeshifter?" I asked.

"I suppose it's better than being a spellcaster," Sin replied.

"Sin is a demon," I explained.

"Oh, well, that makes sense."

I didn't hear even a hint of sarcasm in Faye's voice.

"You don't sound surprised," I remarked.

"I'm not sure much could surprise me today," Faye replied.

"I like her," Sin announced as she bounced toward us. "It's been so boring here while you were gone. I was tempted to go kill the warlock."

"Which warlock?" Faye asked with narrowed eyes.

"Does it matter?" Sin asked.

"There are a few I don't want dead," Faye replied.

"I think Sin is talking about Nicolas," I explained. "You know, I never asked Kaine how many Azureans he brought back with Nicolas."

"Kaine is a fool for not killing Nicolas Verdugo," Faye muttered. "That warlock is going to cause him problems later."

"I take it you know him," I remarked.

"Not really, but I know enough to be wary. I grew up in Azuredale. That's one of the biggest reasons Kaine's family never approved of me. Nicolas is my nephew."

"You're a member of the Verdugo family?"

"No," she replied with a laugh. "The Shadow Walkers would have approved of me if I'd been part of another hunter family. Nicolas's mother is my sister, and she's pure evil."

"Dante told me his father raised them all," I began. "Did Nicolas have more contact with his mother growing up than his brothers did with theirs?"

They all had different mothers, and I knew Dante's mother had only met him once and shown no interest in spending any time with him.

She shook her head. "I'd already moved away, but I hear she saw him a few times. By then, my sister was too far gone to have any involvement with him. Hard as this may seem to believe, I think he would have been worse off with her in his life." Her attention shifted to Sin. "I want you to know that I never approved of what she does. Death magic goes against nature, and I think it may have even warped Nicolas before his birth."

"She's a demon hunter," Sin hissed.

Faye nodded. "Yes, but I'm not. I left to get away from her and the others who were always hanging around."

"Did you ever tell anyone about them?" I asked. "Dante seemed surprised that there were demon hunters in Azuredale."

"I tried, but it's not that easy to convince a bunch of people who don't believe in demons that demon hunters are hiding among them," she explained. "I was the weird outcast in Azuredale, too."

"We should take the warlock with us," Sin announced.

"Kaine?" Faye asked.

"No, Nicolas," Sin replied with a roll of her eyes.

"You're joking, right?" I asked.

"She has to be," Faye stated.

"I'm serious," Sin insisted. "He fascinates me, but now that I know his mother is a demon hunter, I'm torn between wanting to get to know him better and wanting to disembowel him. He's a very interesting warlock."

"He's a dangerous warlock who wants Dante dead," I reminded her.

"I suppose you're right," she agreed with a sigh.

"I'm not sure there was ever a chance for Nicolas to turn out normal with all the death magic used by my sister," Faye remarked.

"Your sister still lives in Azuredale?" I asked.

Faye opened her mouth to reply before closing it and looking away. "It's probably best if we don't talk about her. Just know that death magic takes its toll on a spellcaster. They never come out the same. How long are you planning to stay here?"

"I think Kaine feels it would be best if I stay with you as long as you'll have me now that the other Shadow Walkers know about me," I replied.

"Yes, I know that," she began. "I also know you're not going to stay at the Tulurgate Peninsula. Even if you didn't know how dangerous it is for you here, you'd leave to help your warlock and friends."

I looked away. "I'm not sure what you mean."

"Enough," she said with an exasperated huff. "I'm too tired to stay up and play games. I'm going with you when you leave."

"Why?" I asked.

"It's long past time for me to leave here. I don't belong, but that's not the only reason I plan to go with you. If they figure out who you are, I'll be in a lot of trouble. I don't trust Kaine to keep his promise to protect me. I also want to help you."

"I'm sorry," I told her.

"Don't be," she replied. "As I said, it's time to go. It's time to find a place where I belong. So, when are we leaving?"

"Tomorrow, if I can get the information I need tonight."

"Are you meeting with someone?" she asked.

"Sin is going to help me have a dream meeting with Dante," I explained.

She looked at Sin and then back at me. "I didn't know anything like that was possible. I'm going to pack some supplies and then get some sleep. Don't even think about leaving without me."

"Oh, I won't," I assured her. "I'm not going to turn down any offers of help. Something tells me I'll need all the back-up I can get."

Chapter Ten

I had so much nervous energy that it was hard falling asleep again.

By the time I started to doze off, Sin was getting impatient. She'd suggested knocking me out before I'd reminded her that a head injury would likely delay our departure.

I closed my eyes and steadied my breathing until a cool breeze awakened me. When I opened my eyes and looked around, I was at the edge of the Heathergate Refuge.

I stood and looked for Dante. This had to be our shared dream. They always felt more lucid than regular dreams.

"Dante!" I called out.

"Over here," he said as he raced toward me.

We stopped short of touching, not that we could touch in our dreams.

"It's so good to see you," he whispered.

"Yes, I was starting to worry I wouldn't see you tonight. I had trouble falling asleep," I told him. "This has been a crazy day."

"What's been going on?" he asked.

I shook my head. "Sin will be mad if I get distracted. I

need Nicolas's rotation schedule for the next three days so I know where to find Ambrose. We have to get out of the Tulurgate Peninsula tomorrow."

He looked like he wanted to push for details, but he reined in that urge and gave me the information about where I could find Ambrose if he had indeed taken Nicolas's hunting rotation.

"Now, tell me what's going on," he prompted.

I gave him a brief rundown of the meeting with my grandfather and the dinner at his home.

"Eventually, they're going to figure out I'm not Ella Shadow Walker," I told him. "I think it will be sooner rather than later. They don't trust Nicolas all that much, so I suppose at least I have that going for me."

"I don't know why Kaine didn't kill my brother," Dante mused.

"I can't get a good answer from him," I replied. "I don't know what to think of Kaine. He seems concerned about my safety. It sounds like he grieves my mother's death, but he still kills shapeshifters, and I don't think he feels the least bit guilty about that. I think he views me and my mother as special exceptions, or maybe he thinks of us as more spellcasters than shapeshifters."

"Whatever the reason, I think it's smart not to put your faith in him," Dante replied. "Even if he has your best interests at heart, he's being careless. This situation is so unfair. I had you with me again, and we were so close to safety."

"I know," I agreed with a sigh. "Tell me what's going on with you. Have you had any luck with the perimeter spell? Have you seen my father?"

"No and no," he replied. "We've almost looped around the perimeter and found nothing. I'm not sure we should risk going to your father."

"Much as I want you to tell me he's safe and that you've thwarted my stepmother's plot, I think you may be right to avoid my father. Fiona will back you up, but that doesn't mean my stepmother won't find some way to discredit her."

"Do you really think your stepmother has that much sway over your father?" Dante asked. "We're talking about her trying to kill you. Don't you think your father would listen to those accusations, especially if one of his guards saw you alive?"

"I don't know," I admitted. "Maybe I'm overreacting to all the years he took her side and accused me of exaggerating any problems with her. I feel like it's best to approach him myself, that way, he can't deny that I'm still alive. Has Darius returned since you sent him to talk to my father?"

"No," Dante admitted. "Fiona's worried something went wrong. She thinks he should have come back to find us by now. I think it's possible he doesn't know where we are since we've been moving nearly all day."

"Try to avoid anyone else until I get there," I told him. "I'm going to find a way to get past the barrier."

"We're still hoping this spell will wear off," he replied. "Peony can't have had time to alter the whole spell on a large scale. Whatever she put in these bracelets must be temporary."

"I hope you're right. How is Serena holding up?" I asked.

He smiled. "She's doing better than I am. Leaving Azuredale has been good for her. She's been in constant danger, yet she's blossoming."

"It's because she's had a chance to prove herself," I replied.

"Geori is my only problem."

"What's going on with Geori?" I asked.

"Nothing major," he assured me. "He's not patient, nor is he pleasant to be around when he's feeling impatient. I'm starting to like him, but I'd prefer if he wasn't so moody."

"He's not terribly pleasant under the best of circumstances."

Geori had started to grow on me, but that didn't mean

I'd stopped noticing his moodiness.

I heard Sin's voice in the background, and I frowned.

"What is it?" Dante asked.

"Sin wants me to wake up," I explained. "She's calling me."

He sighed. "Well, at least she didn't jerk you out of the dream. I'll see you soon."

"Soon," I replied as I watched the dream fade away. It looked as if Dante was floating farther from me as he slowly disappeared just before I awoke on the sofa in Faye's front room.

When I looked over, I found Sin watching me from the floor.

"Did you get the information this time?" she asked.

I nodded as I sat up. "Yes, I know where Ambrose should be for the next few days."

"Good," she replied. "We need to go to the prison."

"Why would we want to do that?" I asked.

"I need to talk to the warlock," she explained.

"Which warlock?" I asked, though I already suspected I knew who she meant.

"The son of the demon hunter," she replied.

"Absolutely not! That would be beyond reckless. We need to get some sleep and be ready to leave in the morning."

We were not going to the prison.

Chapter Eleven

Sin was very persuasive.

Twenty minutes later, I was sneaking into the prison with her.

It shouldn't be quite that easy to walk into a prison. They must not have a problem with escapes. There was no guard at the front. Though I felt the spell vibrate along my skin as I entered, it didn't prevent me from going inside, and no one raced out to stop me.

"This is a very bad idea," I grumbled as we walked toward Nicolas's cell.

"You've said that several times already," Sin reminded me. "Do you think I've forgotten how you feel?"

"Maybe I'm hoping you'll suddenly agree with me, and we'll go back to Faye's house. I'm no longer protected by that spell to make me look younger, so this could get us in a lot of trouble."

She waved off my worries. "I can kill anyone who's a problem for us. We'll be fine. I would also like to remind you that we didn't have to break in. We just walked through the front door."

"I think we should do our best to avoid being seen," I replied. "Fighting our way out is a good way to get killed."

"It's very hard to kill a demon," she argued. "Unless we

run into a trained demon hunter, I'll be fine."

"Yes, but I'm not a demon," I reminded her. "It's a lot easier to kill a shapeshifter."

She cocked her head to the side. "True, and Dante wouldn't be happy if I let anything happen to you. I'm also starting to like you, so it might make me sad if you die."

"Does this mean you agree it's best to avoid getting me killed?" I asked.

"I've kept you alive so far," she pointed out.

"But it would be easier to keep me alive if we didn't break into a prison," I stated.

She shrugged. "I'm sure it will work out fine."

I'd argued hard against going to the detention area, but Sin was going with or without me. Letting her go alone seemed like a bad idea. Sin was impulsive, and since I didn't know what she had planned for Nicolas, I wanted to stick by her side to try to keep her from doing something rash.

I wasn't opposed to killing Nicolas. He was pure evil, and I didn't think he'd ever give up on trying to kill Dante, but I worried killing him now would create more problems for us.

As Faye had pointed out, a mysterious murder at the prison would lead to a lockdown while an investigation was done. That would make it impossible for us to slip away any time soon. I suspected she'd been making those arguments more for herself than for me. I hadn't suggested going to the prison to kill Nicolas.

"This is his cell," I told Sin.

She tried the door and frowned when it didn't open.

"They lock the cell doors with a powerful spell," I told her.

"This is so irritating," she grumbled. "Can you open the door?"

"Me?" I asked. "Why would I be able to open it? I'm not a spellcaster or a guard here."

"You are part-spellcaster," she reminded me.

"I still can't open it." I pulled back the panel so she

could see inside. "Here. Now you can talk to him."

I stepped away from the door.

"Warlock?" Sin called out softly. When he didn't answer, she spoke louder. "Wake up, warlock."

"Who are you?" Nicolas's voice was hoarse but stronger than the day before.

"My name is Sin," she replied.

"I know you," he remarked. "You were with my brother. You tried killing me."

She laughed. "If I'd tried killing you, you'd already be dead."

He chuckled weakly. "Arrogant. I like that. What are you? You don't look like anything I've ever seen."

"You don't know what I am?" she asked as she studied him.

"No," he replied. "Your eyes are extraordinary. Is the color the result of a spell?"

"Not a spell," she told him. "So, your mother never told you anything about my kind?"

"My mother?" There was no missing the fear in his voice. "How do you know about my mother?"

"Guess," Sin said with a grin that revealed her small fangs.

"You're a demon." His voice shook ever so slightly.

Sin's grin widened. "So, she told you. I'm surprised you never mentioned this to your brother. Dante didn't know demons existed."

He snorted. "Yeah, like I wanted to tell the world about my mother's crazy obsession with death magic and demons. That would have gone over well."

"So, you kept it hidden because you were afraid of what others would think of you?"

He didn't respond right away, and I began to wonder if he'd say anything. "Why are you here? Did you come to kill me because my mother was a demon hunter?"

"Was?" Sin asked.

"She's gone."

"Dead?" Sin pushed.

"Probably," he replied. "Why do you care so much about my mother? How do you even know about her?"

Sin shrugged. "I have my sources."

"Are you going to tell me why you care so much about her?" he pushed. "I told you she's gone. You don't have to worry about her hunting demons."

"Some creatures attacked a bunch of children recently," Sin began. "Soul eaters. A little birdy told me years ago that they're the remnants of demon hunters. I've been trying to confirm this, and you, being the son of a demon hunter seemed like a good person to ask."

"Where did you see the soul eaters?" he asked urgently.

"You know what they are?" I demanded, forgetting my plan to hide in the shadows.

Nicolas didn't seem surprised by my presence. His gaze met mine, and he didn't have his usual condescending smirk in place. "I take it you've seen them, little cat."

I nodded. "Serena put up a protection spell to keep them away, but we had no idea what they were or why we've never seen anything that looks like that before. You have, haven't you?"

"Yes, I've seen them," he admitted. "Death magic takes its toll on a spellcaster. It goes against the balance of nature and leaves a taint. It's a poison that spreads. It's also an addiction."

"So, the spellcaster needs to kill more to satisfy their cravings," I deduced.

"Killing can give you a rush," Sin said in a breathy voice.

Nicolas flashed her a slight smile. "Yes, it can. In the case of death magic, the spellcaster starts to crave more innocent prey. They change, not just emotionally, but physically. The soul eaters were all once spellcasters."

"How is that even possible?" I asked. "Wouldn't someone have seen them like that before?"

"Others have seen them, but they usually don't survive to tell anyone," he replied. "Their prey sees them, but only before death. Soul eaters travel farther out to hunt to avoid drawing attention to themselves.”

“You never thought to mention that your psycho demon hunter mother’s friends were out killing children?” I demanded.

“Did I ever do anything to make you think I’m a hero?” he asked with a raised eyebrow. “Do I strike you as a warlock who cares about the lives of a few children?”

“Don’t play games,” Sin warned. “I can tell this bothers you, so why didn’t you tell anyone?”

Nicolas raised his shirt to show us the large scars that ran from his collar bone to the waistband on his pants. They looked like they’d come from claw marks. I had similar recently healed wounds.

“When did that happen?” I asked.

“When I was ten,” he replied. “My mother suddenly took an interest in me that year. One day, I showed up to surprise her, but I was the one who was surprised. She’d started to change physically already, and I heard her and the others talking about an attack. They also talked about coming up with a way to kill me without my father finding out. I told my father, but he thought I was making it all up. I reported it to a member of the justice panel. That was a very bad idea. I was lucky to escape with my life.”

“The justice panel member was one of them,” Sin deduced. “They tried killing you.”

“He tried handing me over to a soul eater,” he confirmed. “When I tried telling my father a monster had attacked me, he just kept going on about how the rebel familiars were monsters, and it’s why we hunted them. The justice panel member who betrayed me was found dead a few days later, and I never tried telling anyone about the soul eaters again. What good would it have done when the demon hunters and soul eaters were the only ones who’d have believed me?”

“Do you know what annoys me most about this story?” I asked with my arms crossed in front of my chest.

“Please, enlighten me,” he said in a bored tone.

"You know how traumatic this kind of attack can be on a child," I began bitterly. "Yet you still put Serena through similar trauma. You arranged for a shapeshifter to attack and scar her."

"Serena," he spat out. "She's always been weak. My experience made me stronger and harder, so I figured hers would do the same. I *was* impressed with how she fought the last two times I saw her. She'd be worthy of the Verdugo name if she wasn't a dirty traitor."

"She didn't need childhood trauma to make her strong," I snapped before looking at Sin. "Is there anything else you need from him, or did you just want to confirm your suspicions about the soul eaters?"

"How many demon hunters are there in Azuredale, and what are their names?" Sin asked.

"It's hard to say how many there are," he replied. "The ones I knew about as a child left Azuredale years ago. I think that once they start feeding on children, they can no longer live among spellcasters. My mother left shortly after my attack."

"Why are you being so cooperative?" I asked with narrowed eyes.

"I'm not a monster," he told me.

I snorted. "You've killed shapeshifters, including children. You're cruel and sadistic."

"I'm a hunter," he argued. "I'm just doing my job."

"And I'm sure your mother also justified killing children," Sin added. "I'm also a killer, and I don't feel bad about that. Just embrace that side of yourself and stop pretending it's for noble reasons."

"I have another question," I said before Nicolas could argue with her.

"What's that?" he asked.

"If the demon hunters are spellcasters from Azuredale, then why did it seem like the soul eaters normally speak a different language."

"I'm not sure, but I think it's hard for them to communicate when they're that far gone," he explained.

"All they're thinking about is feeding their addiction to death magic. I can help you protect the children they went after."

"The children are already safe," I argued.

"Are you sure about that?" he asked. "You didn't even know what the soul eaters were before you came to see me."

"Let me guess," I began with my arms crossed in front of my chest. "If I help you escape, you'll promise to help me protect the children."

He snorted. "No, I'm not going anywhere near the soul eaters again. I was going to tell you that they burn fast if you use a magical flame."

"Yeah, I figured that out," I assured him. "Anything else?"

"No," he admitted. "That experience made me want to do everything in my power to avoid ever seeing one again."

I nodded and reached out to close the panel on the cell but paused. "Thank you for giving us information on the soul eaters. When Sin wanted to see you, I thought it was a terrible idea."

"I have brilliant ideas," Sin said with a huff.

Nicolas's gaze remained on me, and his expression turned calculating. "And what are you going to give me? How do you plan to show your gratitude, Juliet?"

Sin moved closer and smiled at him. "You're still breathing, warlock. That's how we're showing our gratitude. The next time I see you, I plan to kill you, but not today. Until we meet again."

I closed the panel and followed Sin out of the prison, feeling more nervous leaving than entering since it seemed there would be more spells to keep people inside.

"Your uncle probably had them put an exception in the spell for you," Sin said when I hesitated at the exit.

I nodded. "Can we go back to Faye's now? I'd like to get a little more sleep before we need to leave."

Sin huffed. "Shapeshifters spend far too much time sleeping."

Chapter Twelve

I got about three hours of sleep before we set out the next day.

Few people were around as Faye drove away from her home.

We'd kept our late-night visit to the prison from Faye. I felt bad about lying to her and worse about putting her in danger. Had I been caught visiting Nicolas, it could have caused a lot of trouble for her.

My guilt didn't mean I regretted letting Sin talk me into going to see Nicolas. Knowing more about what the soul eaters were might help Dante or Serena come up with more ideas for dealing with them in the future. Even Sin might be able to come up with better ways to protect the children now that she'd confirmed her suspicions.

"You seem tired," Faye remarked as we exited the car near the area where we hoped to find Ambrose.

"I didn't sleep very well," I replied honestly.

I opened the back door for Sin to hop out in the form of a large black dog.

"I'm surprised I slept so well," Faye remarked. "Considering what we have planned, I expected to toss and turn all night."

"Thank you for helping me," I told her. "I hope this

doesn't get you into too much trouble."

"Kaine is the only one who'll be upset for more than a day or two about me leaving," she replied. "Your grandparents might be upset when they realize you're gone, but they won't make a big deal out of it."

"What happens if you decide to return to the Tulurgate Peninsula?" I asked. "What are you going to tell my grandparents if they ask to see me? I know you said you needed a change, but this means you can never go back."

"It's long past time for me to leave the Tulurgate Peninsula. Maybe I'll go back to Azuredale. I'm not sure yet. If I return to the Tulurgate Peninsula, I can always say you've gone to stay with relatives in Azuredale. No one will check on my story. Where do you expect to find the Verdugo warlock?"

"It might be best if I meet him alone," I told her.

Sin bumped my side.

"I'll take Sin with me. Ambrose will have even more questions if you're with me. He asks a lot of questions under any circumstance, and we don't have time."

She nodded. "I'll wait by the car, but I'm going after you if you aren't back in thirty minutes. I don't know if we can trust this warlock."

"All right," I agreed.

I started walking with Sin by my side until I came to the spot where Dante said I'd find a trap. He'd insisted that Ambrose, like the other Verdugos, was a creature of habit and checked the traps in a certain order. They'd all hated that Dante occasionally changed up the route if they went out with him.

Crouching behind the bushes, I waited, hoping Ambrose would be handling Nicolas's rotation. Since Nicolas usually hunted with less experienced spellcasters, Dante suspected Ambrose would handle the traps along this path because they caught more shapeshifters in them.

I was grateful that there wasn't a shapeshifter in the trap since I didn't want to have to talk Ambrose into releasing it while I was asking him to help me meet with

Erik and Torrent.

Twenty minutes later, I was starting to wonder if Dante was wrong and there'd been a change to the rotation schedule. I breathed a sigh of relief when I heard footsteps and finally saw Ambrose approaching.

He looked so much like Dante that it made my heart ache some. Though Dante's was longer, they had the same dark brown hair. They also had the same silvery-blue eyes, sharp features, and olive complexion.

Ambrose jerked back when he saw me step out from behind a tree.

At first, he didn't seem to know how to react, but that didn't last long.

"Juliet," he said with a wide smile as he rushed forward and hugged me. "Is Dante with you? I've been so worried since he disappeared."

He released me, and I took two steps back as I shook my head.

"Dante *was* with me, but then we got separated again." I released a frustrated breath. "It feels like the fates are against us. He's safe, at least for now, but I need your help to get to him."

I expected him to ask me a lot of questions before he agreed to help me. Instead, he responded without hesitation. "What do you need from me?"

I told him about our attempt to enter the Heathergate Refuge and how the protection spell had been closed.

"The witch traveling with me is going to come looking for me any minute," I explained. "She gave me thirty minutes, and it's been about that long since I left her. Try not to ask too many questions when she gets here. We need to hurry."

"Is she an Azurean or from the place where Dante was hiding?"

"Neither," I replied. "Well, I suppose she's originally from Azuredale, but she's been living at the Tulurgate Peninsula. She left there with me."

"Why were you there?" he asked.

I hadn't yet told him about being rescued by the Shadow Walkers because it felt strange sharing that detail. "It turns out I am technically a Shadow Walker."

His eyes nearly bugged out of his head. "How is that even possible?"

"It's a long story," I told him. "Kaine Shadow Walker is the reason I got away from Nicolas and the other Azureans."

"Is Nicolas dead?" Ambrose asked.

"No, he's still alive."

"Something that will come back to haunt us," Faye complained as she joined us.

Ambrose's eyes narrowed. "What a lovely sentiment for a mother to have."

"I'm not his mother," Faye argued.

Ambrose snorted. "I may have only been eight the one time I saw you, but I remember you."

"I'm not his mother," Faye repeated. "I'm his aunt. His mother is my sister, and we look a lot alike. I left Azuredale before Nicolas was born."

"It's true," I told Ambrose. "She's involved with Kaine Shadow Walker."

"I *was* involved with him," she corrected me. "I don't know Nicolas, but I've heard the apple didn't fall far from the tree. My sister has always been pure evil."

"What do you need from me?" Ambrose asked after a brief hesitation.

"First, I need to speak to Erik," I explained. "He works at the disposal area."

"Why do you need to talk to Erik?" he asked.

"The spell around the Heathergate Refuge must have closed up because of something in the new bracelets. Erik knows the witch who gave them to me."

Even knowing Peony had likely betrayed us, I wasn't sure about sharing her secret with Ambrose or any other Azurean. It could put many innocent spellcasters in danger.

He nodded. "That shouldn't be hard to arrange."

"I also need to see Torrent," I explained. "I'd like to get his take on what could have happened with the Heathergate Refuge spell, and I'm hoping he can get me another bracelet."

Ambrose looked from one of my wrists to the other. "What happened to the one you got from the spellcaster up north?"

"Kaine probably snapped it off so no one would see it," Faye replied.

"Why would he do that?" Ambrose asked.

"Because he wanted Juliet to stay on the Tulurgate Peninsula," Faye explained. "He loves her, and he thinks it's the best way to protect her."

"Kaine seems to love the spellcaster side of me," I corrected her. "That's not important. Can you help us?"

"How did you know where to find me?" he asked before adding, "I'm going to help you, but I'm curious how you knew where I'd be today. You were waiting for me, right?"

"Dante told me in a shared dream."

Ambrose snorted.

"I know it's hard to believe, but I had some help," I explained. "I can't tell you all the details, but a lot of weird things have happened since Dante's magic somehow bound itself to mine."

"I have so many questions." He seemed to be doing his best to rein in his curiosity. "You have to promise you'll answer them all when we aren't in such a hurry."

"If we ever get that chance," I assured him, not certain I'd see Ambrose again after he arranged the meetings.

"We'll have time," he replied. "I'm going with you to find Dante. First, I need to make an excuse to get out of my rotation so my cousin who's out with me doesn't get suspicious. I'll meet you back here in about two hours."

"Is it safe for us to stay here?" Faye asked.

"Since I'm the one checking these traps and no one else will be out here for two weeks, this is the safest place for you to wait," he replied.

"All right," I agreed. "We'll see you in a couple of hours."

Chapter Thirteen

Dante

"We've looped all the way back around to where we started," Fiona announced.

She was right. We'd gone farther than our original starting point, and we'd found no weak points in the spell keeping us locked inside the Heathergate Refuge.

We were going to have to wait for the spell to weaken on its own. I was certain it would. A spell that had taken multiple spellcasters, and possibly demons, to create couldn't be easily disrupted. It would fight against whatever magic Peony had used.

"Shouldn't the shapeshifter you sent back have come to find us by now?" Serena asked. "I know this is a large area, but I feel like he'd be able to find us if he wanted to."

Fiona looked worried. "He may have run into problems. We don't know who we can trust. I have only a few people who I know couldn't possibly be part of any plot that involved trying to kill Juliet."

"Maybe we should find Juliet's father," I suggested. "Something may have happened since you've been gone."

Sticking close to the perimeter until the spell reopened was the safer option since it would be easier to avoid enemies. Even the shapeshifters Juliet could trust might not welcome outsiders. I still felt torn because I didn't want anything to happen to her father.

"I need to go back," Fiona told us. "I'm worried about leaving you out here. If any of the others run into you, they'll assume you're enemies. They may blame you for the problems with the perimeter spell."

"I wouldn't blame them for making that assumption," Serena agreed. "We showed up, and the spell closed."

"Yeah, we look like the enemies here," Geori replied.

"I'm pretty sure it was our fault," I began. "Indirectly, at least." I looked down at the bracelet on my wrist. "Peony must have done something with the spell she put on these bracelets to close off the perimeter."

"I thought it was your demon friend," Geori remarked.

"So did I," I agreed before telling them the highlights of my dream meetings with Juliet.

Both Fiona and Geori looked skeptical of my story.

"It could have just been a dream," Geori suggested.

I shook my head. "This has happened before, and they feel different from normal dreams."

"Juliet told me about the one she had with Dante the last time they were separated," Serena added. "It's demon magic."

"And you're convinced this demon isn't lying to Juliet about her involvement in disrupting the spell?" Fiona asked. "Perhaps she has an ulterior motive for wanting us trapped on this side that she doesn't want to share with Juliet."

"That's possible," I admitted. "Sin's actions haven't given me any reason to distrust her, but she told me I can't trust any demon."

"All right, so the bracelets may have triggered the spell that locked you in here," Fiona mused. "Why not destroy them?"

"Do you know what will happen if we're on this side of the spell with no bracelet?" I asked her. "Will we be able to leave without the bracelets if the barrier opens?"

She opened her mouth to respond before closing it and pausing to consider the situation. "I don't honestly know. We've never had anyone try leaving without a bracelet since that would be incredibly dangerous, and they might not be able to return."

"But we can definitely leave if we get different bracelets," Geori remarked.

She shrugged. "That might work for you, but I don't know about the spellcasters. The spell was designed to keep them out, and the bracelets we have should only work on shapeshifters. Juliet's mother was able to enter because she's part-shapeshifter, but even then, we worried she'd be locked outside. I don't know what would happen if the spellcasters try leaving with our normal bracelets."

"Then we'll keep the bracelets on," I replied. "I can't risk being trapped in here. Juliet should be on her way, but she has matters to handle first. Now, we need to decide if we're going with you to try to deal with Juliet's stepmother."

"I think we need to stay with Fiona," Serena stated. "Saving Juliet's father is important. The guard who knew there was a plot never returned. That can't be a good sign."

"It doesn't necessarily mean there's a danger to him or anyone else," Fiona pointed out. "If he was unable to get our leader alone, Darius might not have been able to give him the message yet. Our leader has been avoiding everyone since he heard about Juliet's death. I haven't seen him, and neither has Darius."

"That sounds very suspicious," Serena mused.

"Not as much as you might think," Fiona replied. "He changed up his personal guard shortly before Juliet's supposed death. They are the only ones other than Nidia who've spent time around him. He also isolated himself for a few months after Juliet's mother died."

"Do you think they'll send someone out looking for you?" I asked. "It would be careless of them to let you continue patrolling alone."

Fiona shook her head. "Darius likely said I was

trapped on the other side of the spell. That's what I would have done."

"That's smart," I agreed.

"Can you communicate telepathically with Darius or one of the other shapeshifters you trust, like Dante does with Juliet?" Serena asked. "I've heard shapeshifters can do that, especially in animal form."

"You can communicate telepathically with Juliet?" Fiona sounded shocked.

"The spell is blocking my communications with her, but normally I can," I replied.

"That shouldn't be possible," Fiona mused.

"It may have something to do with Juliet's mixed heritage," Serena suggested. "It could be why she was able to channel your spellcaster magic to fight the soul eaters."

"Channel your magic?" Fiona asked. "What's a soul eater?"

"We aren't entirely certain what those are," I admitted. "My magic is joined with Juliet's, but I still don't understand everything about it."

"Her father isn't going to be happy about any of this," Fiona said quietly.

"Are we going back with Fiona?" Geori asked.

"I'm going back alone," Fiona announced. "It's nice that you want to help, but without Juliet here, you'll make matters worse. I'm going to scout around the area to see what's going on and try to get close enough to connect telepathically with Darius. We can't communicate from great distances."

"All right," I agreed. "We'll stay here unless we hear someone coming."

"Okay," she replied. "I'll try to be back here before nightfall, but it may be a day or two."

"Are you sure you don't want me to go with you?" Geori asked. "I doubt many will realize I'm not from here since I'm a shapeshifter with a bracelet. It seems like it would be best if you had some back-up."

"Geori is right," Serena stated.

Fiona hesitated before nodding. "All right. We'll travel in animal form."

Geori nodded and stripped his shirt over his head.

Serena caught his hand, and when he looked at her, she went up on tiptoes to kiss his cheek. "Be careful."

"You too," he replied with a smile before he quickly kissed her lips. "I'll be back soon."

Chapter Fourteen

Waiting around for Fiona and Geori wasn't easy.

I had far too much nervous energy. I wanted to walk the perimeter again.

"Just sit down, Dante!" Serena snapped. "You're getting on my last nerve."

"Sorry," I replied. "I'm so tired of waiting for something to happen."

"We've only been waiting a couple of hours," she reminded me. "I know what we can do!"

"What's that?" I asked.

"You can bathe in the lake."

"Very funny," I said in a dry tone before sniffing my underarm and cringing. "Wow! Okay, a bath is a good idea, though I'm not sure my extra clothes are any cleaner than the ones I'm wearing."

"We'll rinse some clothes and hang them up to dry," she replied. "I'll bathe after you. I'm glad it's warmed up some."

"Me too," I agreed. "I'm still not looking forward to climbing into the cold water, but at least I won't already be freezing before getting in there."

We'd made camp by a lake at the edge of the Ivorfalls border.

"Why do you suppose they call the whole border region the Ivorfalls?" Serena asked. "There are only falls on one side. It seems like a strange name."

"It is," I agreed as I looked around. "I believe this whole area was called the Ivorfalls Region before the creation of the Heathergate Refuge, but don't quote me on that. I've never seen any maps that old."

"That makes sense. I'll stand guard while you bathe," she offered.

I nodded. "You wouldn't happen to have any soap, would you?"

"I do." She dropped her pack and pulled out a small bar. "Don't waste any or lose it. I'll make you go under the water to look for it if you drop it."

I laughed as I walked toward the lake. "I promise I won't lose your soap. Did you ever think we'd be worried about losing something we've always taken for granted?"

"No, a lot has changed," she replied as she turned her back to the lake to give me privacy.

I set the bar of soap on my pack near the edge of the lake, stripped out of my clothes, and waded into the water. It was colder than I'd expected. Once I was thigh deep, I dove under and swam out to try to get used to the temperature.

I could still touch the bottom about twenty feet from the shore. By then, I was more used to the water, so I swam back, only to find three large cats and a coyote sniffing the soap.

"I really need that," I told them as I reached for it. I used my right hand so they could see my bracelet.

There was no way these creatures could be anything other than shapeshifters. They were simply too large. I was counting on the fact that the bracelet would prove I wasn't an enemy.

It worked because they stepped back and continued watching me as I grabbed the soap. I looked up to see where Serena had gone. I'd have expected her to warn me of approaching shapeshifters.

She was still standing guard, but she had a wolf, a large beaver, and a small black bear beside her. Based on her relaxed pose and hand gestures, it didn't appear she was in any danger.

"Thank you," I told the shapeshifters as I backed into the water with the soap. They weren't making any threatening moves, so I figured I might as well finish bathing. With any luck, they wouldn't suddenly become violent.

The bear nearly knocked Serena over when he leaned into her side, but the wolf moved to steady her.

I hurried through my bath since I didn't want to leave Serena to deal with the shapeshifters on her own for long. When I got out, I dried off using my blanket and put on my cleanest clothes.

The cats and coyote followed me to Serena.

"Do you want to bathe now?" I asked her.

"I'm not sure I should," she said as she looked at all the shapeshifters.

"They haven't attacked us, so I think it should be okay," I told her.

The bear growled, making me wonder if he disagreed with my assessment of the situation.

"I don't know about undressing in front of all of them," she admitted.

The coyote's form blurred until a young boy with brown hair and eyes stood before us.

"Why do you care about undressing?" he asked as he gestured to himself.

The others changed forms, and we found ourselves surrounded by children no older than ten.

"I don't undress in front of children," Serena told him.

The children laughed.

"You're funny," the boy who'd been a bear remarked. "What are *you* doing out here?"

Serena met his gaze. "What are you doing out here?"

"I told you we were going to get in trouble, Ellis," a young female complained. "You're supposed to be doing lessons.”

Ellis.

This was Juliet’s brother. He didn’t look anything like her, but I’d heard she resembled her mother. He had dark blond hair and brown eyes.

What were the chances of me running into him?

“I’m tired of lessons and of hearing that I need to become more responsible,” Ellis complained. He didn’t sound petulant so much as mentally and emotionally exhausted.

“You’re the future leader,” another male reminded him.

“I don’t want to be the leader,” Ellis shot back.

“It’s a lot of responsibility for one so young,” I remarked.

“You must feel overwhelmed,” Serena added.

Ellis struggled to compose himself before he spoke again, but I still heard the sadness in his voice. “I’m supposed to pretend my sister didn’t die and start training to be the ruler. It’s not fair.”

“No, it’s not,” Serena agreed.

“Who are you?” Ellis asked. “I don’t remember seeing you before.”

“I’m Dante,” I replied. “I know your sister.”

“You knew Juliet?” Ellis’s gaze remained on me. “Were you good friends?”

“I love her,” I replied.

“I don’t,” Ellis admitted in a small voice. “That sounds awful, doesn’t it? She was my sister, and I’m sad that she died, but I didn’t know her very well. I always wanted to know her better. It’s so unfair that I never got the chance. I guess it’s because she was older.”

“And your mother hates her,” Serena covered her mouth. “Sorry, I shouldn’t have said that.”

“It’s true,” Ellis agreed. “My mother is glad Juliet died because she wanted me to be the leader. She said Juliet would have wanted me dead, but that’s not true. One time, I went out too far into the lake and almost drowned. Juliet saved me. She didn't have to do that. No one even knew she'd followed me out here. All she had to do was walk away and let me die, but she swam out to get me."

"Juliet is very brave," Serena agreed.

Ellis studied her closer. "How did you know Juliet? And why do you keep talking like she's still alive? I don't know either of you."

The female right beside him smacked his arm. "Knock it off, Ellis. You don't know all that many of the adults here, and how many of Juliet's friends did you know? You didn't know anything about Juliet."

"Stop saying that!" Ellis shouted. "I know I didn't know my sister. She would have been a much better leader. I can't be the leader."

Serena placed a hand on his arm. "You're still young. How can you possibly know you won't make a good leader?"

"She's right," I agreed.

"I hate being forced to train and learn stuff all the time," he complained. "Why can't I play with my friends? Juliet never minded any of that. She wanted to be my father's heir."

I shook my head. "Juliet had no interest in ruling your people when I first met her. I don't think that changed so much as she realized it was her responsibility. It's okay if you don't feel like you can be the leader now."

"His mother says he needs to be ready to take over soon," another male told me.

"Soon?" Serena asked. "You won't take on that role until you're twenty-five. You must have at least fifteen years to prepare."

"Sixteen," Ellis replied with a pout. "My father's been sick since my sister died. Everyone says his heart is broken."

"Sick?" I asked suspiciously.

Ellis nodded. "He's getting worse all the time. I haven't seen him since my mother moved him to have a healer look after him, but she says he's not getting better. Don't tell anyone I told you," he quickly added. "It's a secret because I guess people will worry. You won't tell anyone else, will you? My mother would be really angry with me."

"It's okay, Ellis," Serena assured him. "We aren't going to do anything to get you in trouble. It might be best if we all pretend we never saw each other."

"Yeah," Ellis agreed quietly. "My mother will be upset if she finds out I was talking to Juliet's friends." He looked between us as he asked, "Do you think my sister loved me?"

"Yes," I replied. "I know you're not supposed to talk about it, but can you tell us anything else about your father's illness? We may be able to come up with a way to help him."

"Really?" Ellis asked. "You want to save my father?"

The female rolled her eyes. "He's their leader, too, so of course, they want to save him."

"I'm not sure I can save him, but I may be able to come up with some ideas," I told him. "I don't want to get your hopes up, so that's all I can promise."

"That's more than the healer who saw him was able to do," Ellis grumbled.

"You might want to keep this from the healer," Serena suggested. "You don't want the others knowing we met."

He nodded.

"So, what's going on with your father?" I asked.

"When he first heard about Juliet dying, he was mad," Ellis explained. "You remember, right?"

"Anger certainly makes sense," I agreed, not exactly answering his question. I was doing my best to avoid lying to him too much.

"He was even going to go to the trading post to see if he could find any sign of the rebels along the way." Ellis paused and looked at his friends. "Don't tell anyone I mentioned that. My mother says it could be a problem for my father and her. The day he was supposed to go, he was tired, and he didn't get out of bed. My mother wouldn't let me see him because she said he wanted to be alone. I've only seen him once since then. He's lost a lot of weight, and he has trouble eating. His skin is grayish with a slight green tint to it."

"Grayish green?" Serena asked, latching onto that detail just as I had.

Ellis nodded. "Yeah, I've never seen anyone look like that, but my mother and the healer said it's part of his sadness."

"I never heard of sadness making anyone green," a male scoffed.

I hadn't either, but I knew some spells could.

"Any other symptoms?" Serena asked.

He shook his head. "It's hopeless, isn't it? I don't know how to make him happy again, and the healer says that's the only cure. They won't even let me see him since they moved him."

"Have you seen Fiona or Darius?" I asked.

"They're out on patrol," he replied. "I don't think they'll be back for a few days. I guess there's something big going on at the perimeter, but they don't tell us anything."

I nodded. "They probably don't want to worry you."

"Well, it's not working since I'm plenty worried," Ellis grumbled. "If you find a way to save my father, I promise you'll be rewarded."

"We're going to do our best to come up with a way to save him," Serena assured him.

"We need to go back now," Ellis replied. "I guess I'll see you around."

The children all changed forms and ran off.

"Nidia is using a spell to poison Juliet's father," Serena spat out. "She's going to make it look like he couldn't handle losing his daughter."

"Yes, and I'm not entirely sure what we can do about it," I admitted. "It could be one of about half a dozen spells that I know of, but I'm no healer."

Serena sighed. "I wish I'd inherited a talent for healing from my mother's family."

"We need help from outside the Heathergate Refuge,"

I began. "Someone from one of the trading posts must have sold Juliet's stepmother some kind of magical poison. There has to be a counterspell. We need a spellcaster healer."

"She could have gotten the poison from Peony," Serena suggested. "Remember, Peony said they sometimes trade with the Heathergate Refuge."

I nodded. "That's entirely possible. In fact, I think it's more likely than one of the Azureans selling her the spell."

"That demon is going to pay. I'm not letting Peony or Juliet's stepmother get away with this," Serena stated.

I nodded. "One way or another, they will both pay. Hopefully, I have another shared dream with Juliet tonight so I can tell her what we learned. Since it looks like we'll be waiting here for a while, I think we should set up a perimeter spell so no one else sneaks up on us."

Chapter Fifteen

Juliet

The meeting with Erik was the easiest to arrange, so that's what Ambrose worked on first. He didn't know if Torrent would be willing to see him since their families weren't close.

Ambrose got out of finishing his rotation with his cousin as promised. Apparently, no one was ever surprised when he shirked his responsibilities, so they didn't even ask where he was going.

"I never considered how useful being unreliable could be," I mused as I waited with Ambrose, Faye, and Sin at a small clearing south of the disposal center.

Ambrose grinned. "Few realize how great it is being the one no one can count on."

"I didn't say no one can count on you," I told him. "When I needed help, I immediately decided to go to you."

He laughed. "That was your mistake."

"You aren't unreliable," Faye argued. "You skip out on the responsibilities that don't matter to avoid having anyone count on you for anything too important, but you come through when it really counts."

"How do you know that?" Ambrose asked. "You don't

even know me."

"I've heard enough about you," she replied. "Since my nephew is a Verdugo, I've kept up on what goes on with your family. Your antics have always been entertaining."

"Juliet Shadow Walker," Erik said as he approached us. "Why did you ask to meet me?"

Standing a couple of inches over six-feet-tall, with long blond hair, full lips, and deep blue eyes, he was almost pretty, as Sin had described him.

"Why do you keep calling me Juliet Shadow Walker?"

He shrugged. "It's the name you were using when we met. Ambrose said you urgently needed my help. Where's Dante?"

"That demon you call your ally trapped him in the Heathergate Refuge," I replied angrily. "The bracelets must have triggered something that locked the protection spell down. I can't get in. Dante can't get out."

"The bracelets can't do that," Erik argued.

"Oh, they can," Sin insisted as she prowled closer. "I'm a very unhappy demon. Being made a fool of does that to me. You see, I believed Peony had either changed or was smart enough to know it was a bad idea to mess with me."

"Peony wouldn't do something like this," Erik argued. "What reason could she possibly have for betraying you?"

"I don't know," Sin replied. "Maybe she was afraid we'd tell you all about her past."

"What's to know?" Erik asked. "She was cast out for breaking a few rules."

"First, she wasn't cast out," Sin stated.

"Second, she was using death magic," I added.

Erik blinked twice, looking as if he wasn't sure he'd heard me correctly. Finally, he shook his head. "Impossible. I would know if she was using death magic."

"How would you know?" I demanded. "We've recently discovered that spellcasters living among the Azureans are also using death magic."

Erik tensed. "Who told you that?"

"My sister was one of them," Faye replied. "I knew

about it before I left Azuredale."

I felt his magic surge as Erik's expression changed. No longer did he look like the sweet, shy warlock who'd ineptly flirted with me at the disposal center.

"You're one of them," I hissed.

His shocked expression was obviously faked as his magic continued to build. The dark energy sent chills down my spine. "I don't know what you're talking about. I'm a friend to the shapeshifters at the Heathergate Refuge."

"But not to demons other than Peony," I accused.

"Demon hunter," Sin spat out.

Ambrose hadn't said a word. I didn't know what he was doing, though I could feel his power. He kept it close to him, unlike Erik.

Erik laughed. "You found me out. Oh well, you'll all be dead soon. I really am sorry, Juliet. I had hoped we'd simply trap you in the Heathergate Refuge. Peony wanted you there so your stepmother could kill you, but I hoped you'd survive and never return. Sadly, now, I have no choice but to kill you."

I felt the magic around us intensify as about a dozen hooded spellcasters emerged from the trees surrounding us. They must have used some sort of spell to cloak their presence. I hadn't heard them until they were almost upon us.

Sin shifted to dog form and growled low in her throat when she saw them. She moved closer to my side, and I could practically feel her tension, not that I blamed her.

"Why am I surprised?" Ambrose spat out as he glared at Erik. "You've been lying about being in league with a demon for years."

"A demon in league with demon hunters," I added. "That's low."

"Funny what a demon will do when she's been betrayed," Erik replied with a laugh. "She's the one who taught us how to harness demon energy to make us stronger. She also taught us the power of death magic. I'm going to enjoy draining the last of your power, Juliet. You are a fascinating creature with energy like none I've ever seen."

"I guess you don't feel that bad about having to kill me," I spat out.

He grinned. "No, I've killed too many to feel any guilt."

"You're willing to risk turning into a soul eater?" Faye asked.

Erik waved off her words. "That only happens to those who get too greedy. If it happened to everyone, we'd have been discovered long ago. I take just enough to make me stronger. Enough talk, it's time for you all to die."

I took a defensive stance, expecting them to attack us, but not one moved.

Magic swirled around us, and I immediately recognized the dark magic that had touched on my bond with Dante the day the demon hunters attacked him. It fogged my vision, and when I gasped, I felt it fill my lungs.

Ambrose and Faye both seemed focused on the energy around us, trying to find a way to combat it.

Faye caught my hand. "Don't panic, Juliet. If we can break the spell's hold on us, attack them."

I nodded, unable to speak.

The magic grew thicker around me, and I started to feel like I was being dragged down to the ground.

We were going to die.

Chapter Sixteen

In the distance, I heard the howls of wolves.

Screams followed, and I felt the magic around me ease enough that I could take in my surroundings.

I don't know how they found us, but Alaric and five other shapeshifters in wolf form attacked the demon hunters. The magical hold of six demon hunters was broken as the others struggled to maintain their focus.

I fought my way forward, determined to join the fight. The other shapeshifters didn't seem nearly as affected by the dark magic. It had to be my spellcaster side reacting to the death magic.

A bright light flashed through the clearing, forcing me to shield my eyes and the wolves to yelp. I worried it was another attack from the demon hunters until I saw several had dropped to their knees. They were struggling to their feet when I heard a familiar voice.

"Don't even think about trying anything," Kaine warned. "We'll kill you where you stand."

My vision cleared enough to see Kaine standing with Calista and Nicolas by his side. I had no idea why Nicolas was with them, but I decided to focus on one threat at a time. The demon hunters were the biggest danger, and Nicolas seemed to be working with Kaine, at least for the time being.

Nicolas appeared to have a fresh bruise that stood out against his olive complexion, making me wonder if he wasn't there willingly. His dark blonde hair was messy, and his blue eyes sparkled with anticipation of the fight.

"Do you truly think you can beat us?" Erik scoffed at Kaine. "You're powerful, but you're no match for us."

While his attention was on Kaine, I lunged at Erik and took him to the ground. Before he could draw on any of his magic, I straddled him and punched him. The shapeshifters resumed their attack on the demon hunters.

"Don't let them start working their magic again," I called out to the others.

I didn't have time to see what the others were doing because Erik had regained enough of his senses to roll and pin me beneath him. His fingers closed around my wrists as he pressed them to the ground beside my head.

"It's too bad I can't keep you," he said as he leaned closer and brushed his lips against my cheek.

"Get off of her," Nicolas snarled as he caught Erik from behind and yanked him off of me.

I stood and focused on the other demon hunters still standing while Nicolas dealt with Erik.

Sin was in human form and had a female demon hunter pressed against a tree. I saw blue sparks coming from Sin's hand as the demon hunter screamed while her skin sizzled.

All but one demon hunter was engaged in battle, and that one was about to hit Kaine from behind. I rushed forward and landed a side kick that nearly took him to the ground.

He growled low in his throat, sounding feral as he lunged at me. I pivoted and then spun to kick him again. I could feel him trying to gather his energy for a magical attack, but I wasn't going to give him a chance. I pulled the knife from my sheath and slashed his arm.

He howled in pain. "You're going to beg for death before we're done draining you."

I snorted as I held the knife and took a defensive stance.

"In case you missed it, your side is losing. You might want to reconsider your alliances and beg the Verdugos and Shadow Walkers for mercy," I told him.

He sneered at me. "Mercy? Only the weak show mercy. That's what you are, and that's why you'll die."

"If we're weak, then why are you losing?" I taunted. "Why are you staying back like a coward?"

He lunged at me again, and I brought the knife up beneath his ribs.

A gurgling whimper came from him as he grabbed my wrist to try to pull my hand and the knife away.

I yanked the knife out and jumped back as he released my wrist. Rather than immediately dropping to the ground, he stumbled toward me, so I kicked him to knock him back. He tried to stand, but he didn't have the energy with the blood pooling around him.

When I looked around, all but three of the demon hunters were dead. Those that were still alive were all subdued.

Two wolves were injured, and Ambrose had a gash on his forehead.

"Where is Serena?" Alaric demanded in my mind.

I released a tired breath and replied, *"She's at the Heathergate Refuge. Something went wrong with the perimeter spell, and we got separated."*

"Are you communicating with the wolves?" Faye asked as she came up beside me.

"One of them," I replied before looking at Kaine. "How did you find me?"

"Nicolas was given a spell to track your bracelets," Kaine explained.

"But you took the bracelet from me," I reminded him.

He flashed me a guilty smile. "I had a small piece of it melted into the buckle on your boots in case I needed to use it. I worried you'd leave."

I looked down at my boots and frowned. "Great. Now

you've ruined my boots. I'm not walking around with anything Nicolas can use to track me."

"It's a good thing I can track you," Nicolas snapped. "You'd already be dead if I hadn't shown up."

"Why did you save me?" I asked. "Let me guess. You're still hoping to have me as your familiar. Or are you hoping I'll lead you to Dante?"

"We came to an agreement that allowed Nicolas to earn his freedom," Kaine explained.

"I'm more interested in destroying demon hunters than owning you," Nicolas added.

I didn't trust him, but I'd worry about that later. My attention shifted to Alaric, who was still in wolf form. "And how did you find me?"

"It was an accident," Alaric replied. *"We were hunting when I caught your scent, and I wanted to check on Serena and Geori. I don't see him either."*

"Only Sin and I were left outside when the perimeter spell locked. We need to get back in there." My attention shifted to Erik. "How do we break whatever spell Peony put on the Heathergate Refuge?"

Erik still looked defiant, even sitting on the ground with his hands tied behind his back. "How would I know? It's not my spell."

Nicolas pulled back his foot and kicked Erik's back. "Answer her question, or I'll beat the answer out of you. I've had a rough week, so I'd prefer if you take the last option. You're the one who gave me the tracking spell, so you had something to do with those bracelets."

"I'm telling you the truth," Erik said with a groan. "It's not my spell. Peony gave me the tracking spell, and I passed it on to you."

"We need to go see the demon who made the bracelets," Kaine stated.

"That seems like the only way to get answers," Ambrose agreed as he wiped blood from his forehead. "Though I'm still not sure I believe these spellcasters don't know more."

"Even if they know more, we need the demon to break the spell," Kaine pointed out.

"I'm going to destroy her," Sin said with a sweet smile. "I should have done it more than a hundred years ago."

"Don't kill her until we know how to get into the Heathergate Refuge," I warned.

Sin glared at me for several tense moments before nodding. "Fine, we'll get the information we need, and then I'll destroy her."

Chapter Seventeen

Our biggest disagreement was over who would go with us to deal with Peony. Someone needed to take Erik and the other surviving demon hunters back to Azuredale and make sure they were questioned so any other Azureans practicing death magic could be dealt with.

After much arguing, Faye agreed to take them back. Kaine called in two other Shadow Walkers. It would have been better to have someone currently from Azuredale travel with them, but Ambrose refused to leave until he knew Dante and Serena were safe. No one trusted Nicolas.

Nicolas was a big problem.

"So, you kept him alive in case you needed him to track me?" I asked bitterly as I walked beside Kaine to where the vehicles were parked.

"Yes," he replied, not sounding the least bit guilty about his choice. "I hoped you'd be smart and stay at the Tulurgate Peninsula where you belong, but I suspected you'd run. Faye helping you was unexpected."

I did nothing to mask my anger. "How can you possibly think I belong there? Your father wanted my mother dead, and I'm sure he'd feel the same about me if he knew the truth."

He stopped walking and met my gaze. "Remind me again, how did you end up in Azuredale? Am I remembering this wrong, or did shapeshifters put you in a trap to get you out of the way?"

"That's different," I argued, though I wasn't entirely certain how others at the Heathergate Refuge would react to my mixed heritage.

My father had kept the truth about my mother a secret from just about everyone as near as I could tell. I still didn't know how he'd convinced the others she was a member of our community, but no one I knew had ever questioned my heritage.

Would my people have accepted my mother or me if they'd known the truth?

I'd find out soon enough since I didn't plan to keep it a secret once I returned home. I intended to learn more about what it meant to be part-spellcaster.

"So, you don't think any of the shapeshifters will want you dead when they realize you're part-spellcaster?" he asked.

"Juliet is good at changing how people see the world," Ambrose said, having been close enough to overhear us.

I snorted. "Yeah, right. That's why you were out hunting."

"He's not too bad for a warlock," Alaric argued as he joined our group. "We were about to try to rescue one of our people earlier today when we saw the warlock let her go." He'd slipped on a pair of shorts but still wore no shirt or shoes. His light-brown hair was messier than usual.

"You let a shapeshifter go?" I asked in surprise.

"Yeah, well, I've had a problem doing my job since I found out you're a shapeshifter," he admitted. "Every time I see a shapeshifter in a trap, I can't bring them back. I'm on the verge of getting in real trouble for doing such a poor job. So far, I've convinced others that the shapeshifters are avoiding the areas I've been assigned, but that won't work for long."

I reached out and caught his hand, smiling as I

squeezed it. "You aren't all that bad for a warlock."

"He gets praise, and all I get is interrogated," Kaine grumbled. "I'd like to point out that I've saved your life twice."

"I appreciate that," I assured him. "I don't appreciate that you wanted to force me to stay at the Tulurgate Peninsula because of some guilt you seem to feel about what happened with my mother."

"Guilt?" he asked. "Why should I feel guilty? I saved her life."

"You never stood up for her, and you continue to hunt shapeshifters," I reminded him. "Or are you going to tell me you've been letting them go?"

"You and your mother aren't like these shapeshifters," he said as he gestured to Alaric and the others.

Alaric snorted. "And you wonder why Juliet doesn't like you."

"I never said I don't like him," I told Alaric.

"She doesn't like how he acts," Ambrose added.

"My feelings for you are complex," I explained to Kaine. "You're my uncle, and you have risked a lot to help me. I'm still mad that you lied to me and made it possible to track me."

"You might be dead if I hadn't," Kaine pointed out.

"Yes, I know," I agreed. "It doesn't make me feel any less violated. I don't think I can have a real relationship with someone who can't accept shapeshifters." My gaze shifted to Alaric briefly. "The same goes for someone who can't accept spellcasters."

I started walking again. We needed to get to Peony.

"Do you think Erik sent anyone to warn the demon?" Ambrose asked.

"It's possible," I replied.

"No, he didn't," Nicolas said, having just moved closer to us with Calista and Sin by his side.

"What makes you say that?" Ambrose asked.

"Erik wants to be the hero and kill you," Nicolas explained. "He wouldn't want someone else to tell the demon. He'd want to brag about his accomplishment."

"Let me get this straight," Kaine began with narrowed eyes. "The son of a demon hunter is telling us that we have no reason to worry. We're supposed to trust you?"

Nicolas shrugged. "You can doubt me if you want. I'm telling you how I would have played it. I would never have sent someone else to tell the demon because they might have taken credit for my work. Erik wanted to look good. Who could blame him? He's low-ranking in Azuredale, and no one respects his family."

"Your reasoning makes sense," I agreed. "I still don't think we should assume Peony hasn't been warned."

"Yes, we need to be prepared for a possible ambush," Kaine agreed.

"Why?" Sin asked. "Peony will have no reason to think you and one spellcaster could have defeated her demon hunters. Erik would have only been expecting the two of you unless he was warned there would be more."

Ambrose shook his head. "She's right. I only told Erik you were with me. He probably thought it would be easy to handle us."

"Let's hope you're right, and we can take her by surprise," I replied.

Chapter Eighteen

The trip to Peony's settlement was much faster this time since we didn't have to travel the whole way on foot. We stopped about a mile away because the only safe path for vehicles was more likely to be heavily guarded.

We took a trail that went around the back side of the creek as Alaric and the rebels scouted ahead and handled the few guards they came across before we reached them.

Sin was in human form, and I kept having to remind her that we needed to be quiet. Silence wasn't something Sin excelled at.

"Do you need to talk to her for very long before I destroy her?" Sin asked.

"I'm not sure how long we'll need to talk to her. We have to find out how to get past the Ivorfalls border before you kill her," I replied.

"Kill her?" Sin asked.

"You said you were going to kill her," I reminded her.

Sin shook her head. "I'm going to destroy her body and any essence of her being so she can never return to this or any realm."

Nicolas chuckled softly. "I really like you, Sin."

She grinned at him. "I like you, too, though I'm still probably going to make you suffer a slow and painful death after what you did to your brother. I like him more."

Nicolas didn't look in any way offended. "Yes, you've mentioned that before. I'll have to change your mind."

"Could everyone please shut up?" Kaine asked irritably. "If we aren't careful, we'll all end up dead."

"That reminds me," Calista began. "I need some herbs that grow up here to deal with the injuries the two shapeshifters sustained. The wolves seem to be healing quickly, but they're still limping."

"You're a healer?" Ambrose asked.

"Quiet!" Kaine hissed.

I resisted the temptation to ask another question to get on Kaine's nerves. He was right about us needing to stay silent.

Everyone remained quiet as we traveled the last stretch to the creek. Nicolas moved to the back of our group since we weren't sure if Peony knew anything about who Erik had given the tracking spell to.

We'd need to cross the shallow creek to make it to the settlement.

That's where we met Peony. She was standing knee-deep in the creek, reaching under the water for something. The ends of her blonde hair were beneath the surface. No one else appeared to be around. Her blue eyes widened when they landed on me.

"I thought you'd already be back at the Heathergate Refuge," she said as she stood and shook the water off her hands, having apparently not grabbed what she was looking for. "Did you decide to wait until I could get you the other five bracelets? I can probably make another four for you today, but I'll never be able to make enough for a group this size."

She turned and walked to the opposite side of the creek without waiting for a response.

"I'm here about the bracelets you gave us," I told her. "Something strange happened when we tried to enter the Heathergate Refuge."

"Oh, dear," Peony began, not making any effort to

sound genuine. "Did you have trouble crossing?"

"We were ambushed," I replied.

"That's terrible," she said in a bored tone.

"Yes, you sound horribly distraught. What did you do to the spell around the Heathergate Refuge?" I demanded. "I don't have time to play games with you."

She laughed and shook her head. "Stupid shapeshifter. All you had to do was go to the other side with your friends, and you'd have been safe. I was trying to protect you."

"By making sure a spellcaster who wanted me and my friends dead could track us?" I asked.

"Fine," she admitted with a huff. "I didn't care if you died, but you should still appreciate that I gave you a fighting chance. All you had to do was make it into the Heathergate Refuge before the barrier closed. It looks like you survived, so why are you mad?"

"You tried to kill my friends," Sin hissed.

Peony looked uneasy. "Friends? You have no friends. Next week you could be fascinated with their enemies and helping them. These mortal creatures are nothing more than toys, and you know it."

"That's largely true," Sin agreed, "though I had grown bored of playing with mortals. This situation started as a curiosity, but I genuinely like these creatures. They *are* my friends, and you tried killing them all so you could cover up what you're doing out here."

"Don't pretend you believed I'd given up using death magic," Peony snapped. "For that matter, don't pretend you've never dabbled."

Sin quirked an eyebrow. "I'm pretending no such thing. My assumption was that you were lying to the spellcasters living here and doing this behind their backs. I had no idea you were sending out hunters to kill other demons. In case you hadn't guessed already, I'd have destroyed you for that alone."

Peony laughed. "Do you think you have a chance of winning against me? If I were you, I'd turn around and go back to your hiding spot on Reaper Ridge."

"Why is that?" Sin asked in a bored tone.

"Because I'm the one who controls the demon hunters," Peony replied with a triumphant smile. "Death magic is stronger, and you're outnumbered."

"You don't believe that," Sin accused. "You're scared."

"I have nothing to be afraid of," Peony hissed. "You need something from me, and that gives me a bargaining chip."

I suspected Peony didn't feel all that confident in her ability to win in a fight. It's why she was giving so many reasons Sin couldn't kill her. The demon hoped her bluster would make Sin back down.

"What could you possibly offer that would convince me to spare your miserable existence?" Sin asked with a laugh.

"You can't get to your *friends* in the Heathergate Refuge without me," Peony taunted. "My magic, fueled by the death of powerful demons, trapped your *friends*. I'm the only one who can open the barrier."

"That's not possible," Ambrose said from my side.

I didn't think he was talking to Peony so much as working something through in his mind. Peony and Sin hadn't noticed he'd spoken since they were busy squaring off.

"No, it's not," Calista agreed.

I glanced at Ambrose.

"It's too much territory," Ambrose explained.

"Someone would need to walk the whole perimeter to alter the spell," Calista added. "She couldn't have made a change this big remotely."

"So, you're saying we should be able to enter the Heathergate Refuge from a different spot?" I asked.

Ambrose shook his head. "No, I'm saying she's feeding power into the spell to keep this temporary change in place. It has to be draining a lot of her energy along with that of others here. That must be why it was so easy defeating those demon hunters."

"Easy?" I asked. "You call that easy?"

"It *was* too easy," Nicolas agreed, and I nearly jumped out of my skin because I hadn't realized he'd moved so much closer.

When I glared at him, he smirked.

"Did I frighten you?" he asked in a condescending tone.

"Knock it off, Nicolas," Ambrose warned. "You're on our side, at least, for now."

Nicolas sighed. "If the blonde demon dies, the change to the Heathergate Refuge spell will be broken."

Sin was halfway across the creek, and none of the demon hunters had yet to arrive to help Peony. The wolves had started moving farther down the stream to cross. I'd reluctantly agreed to stay with the spellcasters because it was easier than arguing with my uncle.

They felt they would have a better chance of fighting the dark magic if they had some distance between them and the demon hunters.

We were pinning our hopes on three things.

Sin being able to beat Peony.

There not being too many demon hunters.

We were also hoping the help Ambrose had called would arrive.

With any luck, our back-up wouldn't turn on us and try to capture me or the rebel shapeshifters after the fight. I agreed with Ambrose that they'd likely see the demon hunters as the biggest threat and work with us to eliminate them first. I was uneasy about what would happen after the demon hunters were defeated.

Sin made it to the middle of the creek before she froze. Her body stiffened, and when she looked back at us, I could see her mouth open as if to scream.

"She put a spell in the creek!" I shouted. "That's what she was doing when we arrived!"

Peony laughed. "You're almost as dumb as this demon. Poor Sin," she crooned. "You always believed you were so much more powerful than me, but look at you now. You're going to die, and I'm going to have all of your power."

Chapter Nineteen

Sin looked like she was in excruciating pain as she continued to watch me. I didn't know what I could do in a fight against Peony, but I refused to leave Sin at her mercy.

"We have to help her," I told the others.

I started forward, but Kaine caught my arm. "We don't know how that spell will affect us, and we can't help anyone if we all die."

He was right, but I had to do something.

I could still feel the pieces of Dante's magic that were a part of our bond, and I hoped I'd be able to use them to activate some of my spellcaster magic; though I wasn't sure what I'd do, it was all I had.

As I tried to pull on every bit of Dante's magic at my disposal, one of my shapeshifter skills proved more useful.

Still looking at me, Sin fought to get one word out.

"Tazmoranah."

No one else heard her since her voice was little more than a whisper. Even the demon on the other side didn't hear over her own laughter.

My brow knit in confusion since I had no clue what that word meant.

Was it part of a spell?

"Her name," Sin forced out. "Power."

Of course!

I suspected Peony didn't know Sin's real name since none of the demon hunters had used it. Sin had more power, and she'd given it to me.

"Tazmoranah!" I shouted.

The demon went silent, her face reflecting terror that she quickly masked.

"You're too late," she spat out. "Kill them!"

The demon hunters who'd been hiding as they awaited Peony's command emerged, and their dark power started to swirl through the air.

Behind me, the spellcasters sent bright flashes of magic their way to try to disrupt the death magic. Hopefully, the shapeshifters arrived soon to join the fight. I worried they might be caught in whatever spell was affecting Sin, but there was nothing I could do about that now. Instead, I focused on the tool Sin had given me.

"Tazmoranah, you will die today!"

It was a threat, but from the way she suddenly started gagging, I could tell that by using her name, I'd made it more than a threat.

Since the name seemed to be the key to my power over the demon, I continued using it.

"Tazmoranah, release the spell on the creek!"

If Sin could break free from the spell, she could deal with Peony.

Her gaze locked with mine, and I saw hatred burning behind her blue eyes. Her face was tense as she fought my hold over her.

My energy combined with hers in some strange way, though not like with Dante. I didn't feel as if we shared power, so much as I was tethering hers.

Around me, I heard the sounds of the magical battle as if it was far in the distance.

Peony was struggling against my hold on her power. Hot magic shot up the connection, and I cried out as I continued to focus.

"Tazmoranah! Release the spell on the creek!" I

repeated, feeling her magic waiver.

Her name truly was a powerful weapon, so I began to chant it softly, even as she screamed and continued to send angry blasts of energy my way. Some of her attacks made me cry out as my head throbbed. I felt like someone was strumming the nerve endings in every part of my body.

When her power weakened, I had a moment of relief before she sent a blast that knocked me back several feet. I hit the ground, and my breath left me in a loud whoosh.

"Tazmoranah," I continued to chant weakly, even as I heard Sin's cry of rage.

I struggled to a sitting position and watched as Sin and the spellcasters raced across the creek. Calista remained by my side, checking me for injuries. I heard her questions but said nothing more than Tazmoranah's name. I needed to keep her weakened.

The shapeshifters joined the fight with the demon hunters at the same time as I saw several other spellcasters move in behind the demon hunters. I only recognized Laranissa and Torrent, but that was enough to know the newcomers were on our side.

The demon hunters were now slightly outnumbered, but they were still more powerful. The dark energy seemed to be making the spellcasters more sluggish as they struggled to use their magic.

"What are those things?" Calista's voice shook, and my gaze followed the path of hers.

"Soul eaters. Stab them in the eye or set them on fire," I replied before continuing to chant Tazmoranah's name.

I could do nothing more about the three soul eaters approaching us than to give Calista enough information to stay alive and keep the soul eaters from breaking my focus.

She drew a knife and left my side. I hoped others joined her or that she knew some spells that would work.

Sin was still moving slowly when she reached Peony, having been weakened by the spell in the creek.

Peony continued to try to break free of my hold on her as Sin landed a punch to the center of her chest. I heard the crunch of her ribs from across the creek just before Peony screamed.

"You will all die!" Peony shouted as she tried to hit Sin.

Sin laughed and backhanded the demon before calling out to me, "Don't release your hold on her. Keep saying her name."

I did as instructed. Two of the wolves had crossed the creek to help with the soul eaters.

"Come on, Sin," I said as I took a break from my chanting. "Stop playing games and finish it."

I suspected Sin wasn't using magic because she wanted to draw out Peony's death. She was angry and planned to make her enemy suffer before killing her. I didn't know if she failed to realize this was putting me and the others at risk or if she simply didn't care if that was the case.

Whatever her reasons, I needed her to hurry before any of our people were killed. I was starting to feel weaker as Peony fought my hold on her.

Peony's power was also waning, and I felt the instant the spell surrounding the Heathergate Refuge broke.

Dante was in my mind again, comforting me as he added his strength to my hold on Peony.

The demon's scream cut through the air and felt like a knife slicing along my skin.

I cried out in pain, briefly releasing my hold on her.

"*She can't fight you much longer,*" Dante said in my mind.

"*Her screaming is too much,*" I explained. "*There's so much angry magic in the air, all directed at me.*"

"*Just relax.*" Dante's soothing voice in the back of my mind helped ease some of my tension, which caused the pain to recede. "*Draw on my power to help you.*"

"*I'm not sure how. It's simply come to me when I needed it before.*"

"*Focus on pulling the energy into you, and then send it along the line of the demon's power,*" he told me. "*I'll try to push some of my power your way. There must be a way we can control the flow through our bond.*"

I continued my chanting as I tried to focus on my connection with Dante. While concentrating on the bond, I saw the threads of magic swirl around me. I envisioned breathing them into me and having them spread to every cell of my body.

The magic sizzled through me like an electric current. It was exhilarating, and this time when I felt the power move to my hands as it had before, I recognized part of it as my spellcaster magic. It hadn't been only Dante's magic that had helped me kill the soul eater before.

With the surge of spellcaster magic ready to burst free, I shouted. "Tazmoranah, die!"

The magic shot out of me and flowed through my link with the demon. She screamed when the magic hit her, and I saw her blonde hair sizzle.

Sin grinned evilly before slamming her fist into Peony's chest cavity.

Peony gripped Sin's wrist with both hands as her mouth remained open in a silent scream.

I heard the words Sin said, though I couldn't tell anyone what they were later as if the spell was designed to confuse those who might hope to repeat it.

Peony's smooth skin turned redder until it began to mottle. A frothy black substance oozed from her mouth as Sin's hand remained in her chest. Peony's blonde hair turned to ash and floated away in the breeze. Her blue eyes sunk farther into her head as her skin started to look more like red paper that faded to gray before my eyes.

I watched as the demon turned to dust.

Sin stood, still clutching something. She opened her hand and showed me the smooth black stone before tossing it into the creek and falling back.

No longer feeling drained now that I'd pulled on Dante's energy, I raced across the creek to her side just in time to tackle a demon hunter who was about to use an orb spell on Sin.

When he hit the ground, the spell fell from his hand and rolled away.

I felt the demon hunter's dark magic begin to swirl around me, but rather than trying to figure out how to fight him using spellcaster magic fueled by Dante's power, I focused on what I knew.

I slammed my head down, breaking his nose with my forehead.

He howled in pain, and the death magic fluttered around me, no longer controlled by the demon hunter.

I rolled away from him and scrambled to my feet before kicking him in the ribs.

He stumbled to his feet and wiped the blood from his nose before pulling a knife.

I reached for my knife, but he moved faster than any spellcaster should be able to and slashed my arm.

I gripped my bleeding arm and jumped back.

"You're going to die if you don't move out of my way and let me kill that demon who murdered our leader," the demon hunter threatened.

I laughed. "Yeah, as if I'm going to believe you don't plan to kill me no matter what I do."

"There's no reason for you to suffer to protect the demon," he stated, not denying my accusation. "You can die fast and relatively painlessly or suffer a slow, lingering death while you scream and beg for mercy."

"I'll take my chances," I replied as I continued to block his path to Sin. I tried to draw my knife, but he'd injured my right hand, and every time I reached for the hilt, my fingers spasmed.

"You'll regret that choice," he growled as he launched himself at me.

Nicolas was suddenly in front of me, and he spun and kicked the demon hunter before sending a bolt of magic at him.

The demon hunter stumbled back but remained on his feet. Before he could gather the energy for a magical attack, Nicolas lashed out at him with a spell that resembled a purple lightning bolt.

The demon hunter screamed as the spell hit him. He

covered his eyes and dropped the knife.

"Kill him," the demon hunter called out. "Kill the Verdugo."

"Time to die," Nicolas murmured before drawing a knife and plunging it into the heart of the demon hunter.

Nicolas looked around to see that all of the demon hunters were either dead or fleeing the area before turning to look at me. "Are you okay?"

I nodded as I clutched my bleeding arm. "Thanks for your help."

Nicolas laughed. "Did you ever think you'd have me to thank for saving your life, not once but twice?"

"No," I admitted. "We should check on the injured."

I didn't wait for a response before hurrying toward Sin.

Chapter Twenty

Sin was sitting on the ground, hugging her knees to her chest and shivering.

"Are you okay?" I asked as I sat beside her.

She nodded. "That fight used up a lot of energy. I should have destroyed her long ago rather than letting her leave to set up her own community."

"Did you ever imagine she would find so many who supported her use of death magic?"

She thought before responding. "I knew it was possible. Many will do anything for power. What I didn't expect was that she would seek out demon hunters. That was a bold move."

"You sound impressed," I remarked.

"I am," she admitted with no shame. "Of course, she had to be destroyed for her betrayal of all demons and for trying to kill my friends. You're injured."

She sounded surprised, as if she'd just noticed my bleeding arm.

I looked down. "Yes, this is going to make fighting harder."

Sin gripped my wound, and I gasped as her power sizzled through my skin.

When she released my arm, it was completely healed.

"How did you do that?" I asked.

"It's just something I can do with wounds caused by demon magic," she explained. "The blade used on you had a demon spell in it."

"Thank you," I replied. "Will you be okay if I take a moment to contact Dante?"

She stood, and while she still looked shaky, it appeared her strength was quickly returning. Demons seemed to recover faster. She looked down and smoothed out her blood-soaked shirt before nodding. "Yes, I'm feeling much better already."

"If your clothes are an illusion, why are they still bloody? I'm not sure why Peony's blood didn't also turn to dust when she disintegrated."

Evil was the only word to describe her grin. "I like the way the blood of my enemy looks on me."

She moved in the direction of the shapeshifters who were hovering over an injured wolf. Calista was also there. I had no healing talent, so I decided to let Calista and Sin help the wolf.

"Dante?"

His telepathic response came right away.

"Are you okay? You weren't too badly injured in the fighting, were you? I sensed your pain."

"I'm fine," I assured him. *"What's going on at the Heathergate Refuge?"*

He gave me a quick update and told me he was worried about Fiona and Geori, who had yet to return. I was worried but could also see how they might have been delayed.

It was the details of his meeting with Ellis that surprised me. It also made me a little sad. My brother seemed to want to know me better, but that might change once I dealt with Nidia.

Could he ever forgive me if I killed his mother?

"You were right about Ellis," Dante told me.

"I was also wrong," I replied. *"I never thought Ellis hated me or wanted me dead, but I didn't think he'd regret*

not getting to know me better.”

“It's not too late to build a relationship with your brother. Your situation is much different from mine with Nicolas, but I didn't see it until I met Ellis.”

“Nicolas saved my life today. Twice.”

“My brother, Nicolas?”

“Yes, I was also surprised.”

“What was he even doing there?” Dante demanded. “Was he working with the demon hunters?”

“Yes, he was before, but he fought against them today,” I replied. “Kaine, my uncle, brought Nicolas with him to find me.”

“Why did your uncle bring Nicolas with him? He was there when Nicolas attacked us before.”

“Nicolas had a tracking spell to find the bracelets Peony made for us,” I explained. “My uncle needed him to find me.”

“The tracking spell explains a lot,” Dante replied.

“I expected your brother to betray us the first chance he got, and I won't be surprised if he betrays us now. This is a strange situation for me. While I'm grateful to him for saving my life, I still consider him my enemy.”

“He is your enemy,” Dante agreed. “Though he may be less inclined to make an enemy of Kaine Shadow Walker. I've heard that Kaine has been taking over more of his father's responsibilities in the last few years. He is the future head of the Shadow Walker family.”

“I don't trust Kaine,” I admitted. “He hasn't been honest with me, and I'm worried he's going to try to force me to go back to the Tulurgate Peninsula.”

“I want to leave here and find you.” He sounded torn. “It's driving me crazy to be this far from you, but I can't leave the Heathergate Refuge without knowing what's going on with Geori.”

“It's not safe for you and Serena to be out of the protected area right now. There's probably some danger to you at the Heathergate Refuge, but nothing compared to what you would face if the Azureans find you. They're

out looking for Nicolas and the others that went missing, so you have a much greater chance of being captured. I'm going to be heading your way soon, even if I have to steal one of the vehicles to get there."

"I love you," he replied.

"I love you, too."

Chapter Twenty-One

I was washing the blood from my knife as I considered the plan to return to the Heathergate Refuge and help my father.

I'd already cleaned my bloody clothes and discussed my plans to leave with Ambrose away from the others. He was going with me, even though I'd warned him I wouldn't be able to take him past the Ivorfalls.

I still had to talk to Calista since I needed her advice and possibly a healing spell to save my father. That conversation would happen closer to when we left since I suspected she'd tell Kaine what we had planned. He wasn't a fool, so he likely already knew I intended to leave for the Heathergate Refuge, but I didn't want to fight with him about it.

The spell was down, and I was pinning my hopes on the bits of my bracelet left in my boot being able to get me past the Ivorfalls spell. I was hoping the spell in the bracelet still worked now that Peony was dead.

I worried it wouldn't since the change Peony had made to the perimeter spell had died with her, but Sin thought the spell allowing me to enter the Heathergate Refuge would still work. If there wasn't enough power left in the small piece in my boot for me to enter, she'd go in my place.

Torrent approached me with a smile, his dark green gaze fixed on me. His golden hair had been tied back for the fight.

"You know, when Ambrose asked me to meet you, I didn't think we'd be killing distant members of my family who'd developed a fascination with death magic," he remarked.

"Fascination with death magic?" I asked with a quirked eyebrow. "I think that when someone is practicing death magic and hunting demons, you should call it more than a fascination."

"I suppose you're right," he agreed. "This has all been a real shock for us. I'd always heard that some of my family went off to live away from Azuredale because they didn't approve of the familiar practice. None of my family does, but we've never done anything to try to stop it. I guess they just used their disapproval as an excuse to leave."

"That may be why they left initially," I replied. "It may even be why they started using death magic. They could have believed it was a way to fight the Azureans. Who knows?"

"The homes here are still being searched, but a few journals were found, so we may get some answers," he replied. "I'd like to help you get back to Dante."

"You are one of the few spellcasters who may be able to help me," I admitted. "I need a bracelet. It would be nice if I could take some of the other shapeshifters."

He nodded. "Who were you thinking about?"

"I'll have to see which of the shapeshifters want to come with me," I replied. "Alaric wanted to help before, so I know I can count on at least him."

"What about the spellcasters?" he asked. "Are there any of them you want to bring with you?"

I shrugged. "What difference does it make? The demon made a special spell for Dante and Serena, but I know you don't have that ability."

He smiled. "No, I don't, but you have a demon with

you who may be able to lend the necessary magic to make it happen."

I shook my head. "I don't want any of the hunters thinking they can enter the Heathergate Refuge. I can't trust any more spellcasters with the safety of my people. No offense."

He waved off my apology. "None taken. I think it's wise to avoid inviting a bunch of spellcasters into the Heathergate Refuge. You've made some allies, but I don't know how many of them would consider themselves allies of other shapeshifters. I can practically feel the tension between the rebel shapeshifters and the hunters. You especially can't trust Nicolas," he added. "I can't trust Nicolas."

"No one can trust Nicolas," I agreed. "Thank you for helping me. Not just with the bracelets but here with the fighting."

"You're welcome," he replied. "Do you mind if I ask you a personal question?"

"No, but I won't promise to answer it," I told him.

"Fair enough," he agreed. "What are your plans with Dante?"

"Could you be a bit more specific?"

"Are you planning to stay with him at the Heathergate Refuge?" he asked. "Or do you plan to try to find another place to live?"

"I think the Heathergate Refuge is the best option for us," I replied. "Dante and Serena will both be executed if they return to Azuredale, and they risk being captured just about everywhere else. It may not be a permanent solution, but I believe it's safest for now."

He nodded, looking thoughtful. "If that's the case, I may need to find a way to get you those special bracelets for Dante and Serena. I'm not convinced the ones the demon made for them will work much longer. I could be wrong since I have no experience with this variation of the spell."

"I suppose we'll have to figure that out later," I told

him. "When do you think you can have the bracelets for me and the other shapeshifters?"

He grinned. "I have enough for you and any of the shapeshifters who want to go with you."

"You have no idea how glad I am to hear that. I need to get back soon. My stepmother has been poisoning my father."

"I'm sorry to hear that," he replied. "Do you think you'll be able to save him?"

"I don't know, but I have to try."

"I'm going to grab the bracelets while you talk to the other shapeshifters," he said before walking away.

I looked around and found Alaric talking to Ambrose. I started in their direction, but Laranissa stopped me.

She threw her arms around me and hugged me with the same warmth she'd shown after I'd saved Dante from the nāgas.

"Juliet! I'm so happy you're safe."

She grabbed my hand and pulled me farther from the others before speaking again. Her short blonde hair was messy from fighting, and I saw sadness in her dark brown eyes.

"How is Dante? I have been so worried about him since he left my father's home."

"Your father?" I asked. "Is your father the warlock he stayed with on Reaper Ridge?"

She nodded. "That has to stay between us. I'm surprised Dante didn't tell you."

"We didn't have much time together before he got trapped in the Heathergate Refuge," I explained. "He's safe, though I'm concerned he could be hurt or killed if the wrong shapeshifters find him hiding there."

"And Serena?" she asked. "I couldn't believe it when my father told me she was staying with the rebel shapeshifters. She's terrified of all shapeshifters, except for you, of course."

"Serena has handled this better than anyone," I replied with a smile. "She'll be fine. I think she's better off away from Azuredale.”

Laranissa looked sad. “Yes, I failed her.”

She had, but so had everyone else. I didn’t want to add to anyone’s guilt.

“I’m sure you did what you thought was best at the time,” I assured her. “I know you must have a lot of questions, but I need to talk to the other shapeshifters, and then we need to leave for the Heathergate Refuge.”

“I can travel with you to the Ivorfalls,” she offered. “That will give you more back-up in case you run into trouble.”

“Nicolas is my biggest concern, so if you want to help, it would be best if you kept him from following us. If you can find any way to keep Kaine from going after us, that would also help.”

“I’ll do my best,” she assured me.

“Thank you.”

I started to turn to leave, but she hugged me again. This time, she held me close.

“Dante couldn’t have picked a better partner,” she whispered. “He’s lucky to have you.”

“I wouldn’t be alive if he hadn’t found me,” I told her. “I’m the lucky one.”

Chapter Twenty-Two

I'd worried that it would take us several hours, possibly an entire day, to leave for the Heathergate refuge. Thanks to Laranissa's help, I was on the road with Sin, five shapeshifters, and Ambrose in just over an hour.

I even managed to get some healing spells from Calista that might help my father. Without knowing exactly what type of poison he'd been given, Calista had to guess what would work. Two spells in my pocket worked on various poisons, and she seemed to think that one of them would be our best bet. I had a few others that worked only on specific toxins that grew near the demon hunter settlement or the Heathergate Refuge.

We weren't as worried about being stopped, so we took the main road and were able to drive to the edge of the Heathergate Refuge using two vehicles.

I had the new bracelet Torrent had given me on my wrist, and I was going home.

Home.

That word seemed wrong now.

I didn't feel the same sense of dread I had upon approaching the Heathergate Refuge last time, but something still felt off.

When I'd crossed through the perimeter spell the day

my stepmother had betrayed me, I'd been a completely different person. It felt as though years had passed since I'd last seen the place where I'd grown up.

"Are you okay?" Ambrose asked.

"I'm fine," I assured him. "It just feels strange being here again."

The shapeshifters riding with us had already climbed out and were heading over to the vehicle driven by Alaric. Sin had decided to join the others.

"Something tells me you'll feel much better when you're with Dante again," he replied as he reached into the center console and grabbed a phone. "Here, take this with you. I want to be able to talk to my brother."

I took the phone and tucked it into my pack. "I know he'll appreciate this. Leaving you and Laranissa behind has been the hardest part for him. He loves you very much."

"He's my favorite brother," he replied.

"Considering Nicolas is his only competition, I'm not sure that says much."

He chuckled. "Yeah, Dante doesn't have much competition. I guess you'd better go."

"Thank you again, Ambrose," I said before stepping out of the car and heading over to meet Sin and the shapeshifters.

"How far are we from Serena?" Alaric asked, already sounding edgy again.

"I'm going to regret bringing you with me," I said under my breath.

"He promised to behave," Sin reminded me.

"He may even try to keep that promise," Elena added.

"I'm not holding my breath," I stated. "Serena and Dante are close to where they entered the Heathergate Refuge. It's several miles to the east. I decided against having them walk this way to meet us in case Fiona, Geori, or Darius return."

"Why couldn't we drive closer?" Sin asked with an exasperated sigh as we started walking toward the protection spell. "We should have brought another vehicle."

"We couldn't have gotten away with taking another," I told her as I looked back at the three shapeshifters in our one car. "It's going to be hard enough to hide one when we have to start walking to meet the others."

"But we could have gotten closer," Sin complained.

"This is the best place to enter," Alaric answered for me. "Most of the outside perimeter can only be reached on foot, according to the maps."

"You can get in the car," I told her.

Sin shook her head. "You seem uneasy, so I'm going to stay with you in case there's a problem."

Alaric paused at the very edge and looked at the mist surrounding the Heathergate Refuge. "I've never seen anything like this before," he said in awe. "For a moment, I could have sworn I saw a woman beckoning us to enter."

"Morena," I whispered.

"Who?" Alaric asked.

"There's a legend about our original princess," I explained. "When I left, I imagined seeing her in the mist. I think it may be an illusion caused by the spell."

Sin nodded. "The demons involved with the spell thought it would be funny."

We watched as the car moved in front of us and drove through the veil of magic. Energy swirled around it like a vortex before it appeared to vanish into the mist.

"Amazing," Elena whispered.

The spells surrounding the rebel community were nothing like this. Seeing it through the eyes of newcomers, I was able to better appreciate the complexity of the magic.

I worried that it had only taken one demon to disrupt the spell protecting the shapeshifters within. In that case, the spell had locked all others out, but I wondered if it would be possible for a demon to at least temporarily disable the entire spell. I would need to address that potential problem sooner rather than later.

"There's so much to do," I said as we walked into the mist.

"Take it one step at a time."

I didn't know if Alaric was responding to what I'd said or if he was simply giving encouragement to himself as he faced the unnerving sensation of powerful magic surrounding him. I wondered if he regretted his decision to walk rather than ride through.

Once we'd made it past the magic, Alaric and Elena released heavy sighs.

"That was more intense than I expected," Alaric stated.

"Yes," I agreed. "I've only been all the way through one other time, and I was in a truck then. It's more intense on foot."

"We need to head east, right?" Alaric asked.

"Right," I agreed as I headed to the car.

"Are you going to drive?" Alaric asked.

"I don't have much experience driving," I replied. "It will be better if one of you is behind the wheel."

Alaric nodded. "I'll drive, and Elena can ride with us." He looked at the other shapeshifters. "Change forms. You'll travel faster in wolf form."

I pointed east. "This dirt path will get us within five miles of where we need to meet Dante and Serena. Hopefully, Geori will be back by then."

"I can't believe he left Serena unprotected," Alaric grumbled as he slid into the driver's seat. "It was his job to protect her."

"No," I replied. "It was his job to accompany me to save my father. He's not Serena's guard. She doesn't need a guard, you irritating wolf."

"You need to get it together," Elena told him as she climbed into the backseat with Sin.

I slid into the passenger's seat. "She's right. Part of the reason I was so relieved when you didn't go with us before was that you act too erratically around Serena. The closer you get to her now, the more you're only focused on Serena."

I needed to come up with a way to keep him from being too much of a problem once we met up with the others.

One problem at a time.

First, we needed to get to Dante and Serena.

Chapter Twenty-Three

I didn't communicate telepathically as much as I would have liked with Dante during the drive. It was hard resisting the temptation to reach out to his mind, but we all needed to focus on our surroundings.

It hadn't been that long since I'd felt safe everywhere in the Heathergate Refuge. A lot had changed.

About an hour into our journey, we had to park the car and head out on foot. We tried hiding it as best we could so it wouldn't attract the attention of any shapeshifters.

No one spoke much as we put supplies into our packs. The other shapeshifters remained in wolf form. I expected Alaric and Elena to change, but they chose to stay in human form.

"Are you ready to go?" Alaric asked me.

I nodded.

"Do you think we'll run into any traitors?" Elena sounded excited by the prospect. Her blue eyes were alight with eagerness.

"I don't know, but I hope not," I replied.

"Why not?" she asked. "A good fight would do us all some good. Everyone is too tense."

"We just had a good fight. Besides, how will I know if they're traitors?" I asked. "If they weren't with my stepmother the day she betrayed me, then I'll have no way of knowing if we can trust them. That seems like a recipe for disaster."

"She's right," Alaric agreed. "We could end up killing people who are on Juliet's side or trusting those who will try killing us. It's best if we don't see anyone until after we meet up with Serena."

"And figure out where Geori is?" Elena asked.

"Nope, he's focused on Serena," I replied.

Elena nodded. "It's always that way with male shapeshifters when they first find their mate, especially when they fight it."

"Yes," I agreed. "I've seen this reaction with other males."

"Mate?" Alaric asked with an obviously fake laugh. "Serena isn't my mate."

"But you want her to be," Elena stated.

"He'll never let that happen," I pointed out.

"I suppose he can't," Elena replied.

"Why not?" Sin asked.

She'd been quiet for more than an hour, which was unlike her. I'd tried asking her questions but gotten simple one-word answers. "Wait! I remember." She pointed at Alaric. "You think you're too good for Serena."

She skipped ahead.

Alaric glared at her. "I don't think I'm too good for Serena." His gaze shifted to me. "You know that's not the reason."

"I know it doesn't matter what your reasons are. We need to focus on our surroundings. Stop thinking about Serena. What am I even saying?" I asked under my breath. "You probably can't stop thinking about her, but at least try focusing on what we need to get done."

Alaric grumbled something I couldn't quite make out, but I didn't think it mattered. He was a good fighter, and at the very least, he would keep Serena safe.

It was my hope that we wouldn't have much of a fight. If there were too many looking to remove my father from power, then the fight ahead of us would be the least of my problems. It would mean there were a lot of disgruntled shapeshifters who wouldn't simply fall back in line.

Were there that many people unhappy with the current conditions in the Heathergate Refuge?

My stepmother was able to find enough people to help her get me out of the way. Until then, I hadn't considered that there might be a large group of unhappy shapeshifters at the Heathergate Refuge.

"I sense your unease."

Even with my dark thoughts, I felt soothed by Dante's voice in my mind.

"I was considering the possibility that there might be a larger number of traitors among my people than we can deal with."

"Were there a lot of people asking for change?"

His question made me frown because I didn't know the answer. I could blame it on my age, and that *was* part of it. There was also the fact that I'd avoided thinking about anything related to my future as the leader. I'd avoided involving myself in politics whenever possible.

"My father is wrong about me. He has always said I'd make a great leader, but I don't know the first thing about any of the problems my people are facing. I had some ideological beliefs related to the rebels, but I didn't know what they were dealing with until recently."

"You're still young."

"So is Ellis," I replied. *"In fact, he's much younger. I keep parroting what my father said about Ellis not having the temperament to lead. Those are my father's words, not mine."*

"Do you think he'd make a good leader?"

"Not now," I replied. *"He's still a child, and Nidia's influence hasn't been good for him. If she were no longer in his life, maybe he'd make a good ruler someday."*

"I like your brother, from the little time I spent around him," he remarked.

"Do you think he'd make a good leader? I still don't

know if we'll be able to stay here, even if we save my father, and it would make me feel better leaving my people if I knew my brother could someday take my father's place."

"I don't honestly know. He doesn't want the role any more than you did before, but that could change."

"I still don't want to be the ruler," I admitted. *"Maybe my father didn't either."*

"I imagine few are born with the desire to lead," he replied. *"For what it's worth, I think your concerns are a good sign. You feel like you need to know more about your people's problems. You also want to help others. These are all good qualities in a leader."*

"Do you think we'll be able to save my father?"

"That, I also I don't know," he admitted.

Of course, he had no way of knowing. Dante knew less about the state of the people at the Heathergate Refuge than I did, yet I'd still hoped for some reassurance.

I shook off my disappointment at his answer.

It was time to deal with reality. I'd spent enough of my life avoiding facts that might force me to think about my future. Now, I planned to face problems head-on. No matter what I found, I would save my father.

"We're almost there," I told him.

"Thank goddess," he replied. *"I can't wait to hold you again."*

I smiled because no matter what else might happen that day, I'd get to see Dante soon.

Chapter Twenty-Four

We quickly gathered everything we needed and started walking at a faster pace.

Alaric had one other shapeshifter change to human form to help carry gear. We weren't traveling as light as the last time we'd been on foot since we didn't have nearly as far to go. I wanted to make sure we had changes of clothes, food, weapons, and gear to set up camp for the night.

Though I'd hoped we'd reach my father by nightfall, it was beginning to look like we'd need to wait until morning.

The shapeshifters who'd traveled the whole way in wolf form were tired, and the sun was already setting as we neared the spot where we were meeting Dante and Serena. We wouldn't be much good in a fight if we were all exhausted.

Thankfully, it was a relatively quiet trip, and I didn't need to answer many questions. I had too much on my mind to engage in conversation. There was little telepathic communication with Dante beyond updates on when we'd arrive.

Once we were close enough to see the lake ahead, I smiled for the first time in hours.

Dante stood by the edge of the water. When he caught sight of me, he ran toward me.

I raced out to meet him, dropped my pack, and threw myself into his arms.

He lifted me from the ground and swung me in a circle.

"I've missed you so much," he murmured before brushing his lips against mine.

A lot of the tension that had gripped me eased as I finally had the man I loved in my arms again. It went beyond his physical touch; our combined magic also moved around us. When we were apart, it felt like a band stretched to its limit, and that tension carried over to me.

He had yet to set me down, so I asked in a breathy voice, "Are you going to put me down or hold me all day?"

"I want to hold you for the rest of my life," he said in a ragged voice. "Every time I let you go, you're taken from me."

"Oh, Dante," I whispered as I gripped his hair and pulled him closer.

I didn't care that the others were watching and perhaps waiting for me to tell them if this was where we should set up camp. The world could wait a little longer. I needed to kiss Dante as much as I needed my next breath.

His lips lingered on mine as I felt the hum of our magic intensify. All the tension and love I felt poured into that kiss. I wouldn't have thought it possible, but I felt our magic become even more intertwined.

When Dante broke the kiss and set me on my feet, I looked around, and some of the interconnected strands of power were swirling together. It looked as though we were at the center of a magical tornado made of beautiful shades of blue, green, and silver.

The vortex closed in around us, pressing us closer both physically and metaphysically. I could never have envisioned something quite so intense. The humming of energy was loud yet soothing in a surprising way.

When the tendrils of power brushed against us, I sighed softly, feeling almost complete. As I welcomed the magic into me, the swirling slowed, and the tendrils around us grew fainter until I could no longer see them. They were still there, but they were now inside of me—inside of us.

His arms were still wrapped around me, and my hands were on his chest.

"What just happened?" I asked in a shaky voice.

"Your magic fully bound itself to mine." His voice was ragged.

"I could have sworn it had already done that," I remarked as I rested my head against his chest. "Is this how the bond between spellcasters is?"

"Yes," he replied. "I think there are some differences, probably because you're part-shapeshifter."

"I don't know too much about how it feels when a shapeshifter takes a mate," I admitted. "My father never wanted to talk to me about that."

He pulled away and brushed my hair back from my face. "It looks like you really are stuck with me now."

"Was that ever in doubt?" I asked.

"No," he admitted.

"That was the strangest thing I've ever seen," Elena mused, which was when I realized the others had been standing around watching us.

"It was beautiful," Serena whispered.

Dante reluctantly released me, and when I stepped back, Serena hugged me.

She didn't look much different from when I'd first met her. She still had the same long, curly black hair. Her olive complexion and silvery-blue eyes were the same as Dante's. The biggest change was in the confident way she now carried herself. No longer did she clutch a knife and look around as if afraid she'd be attacked.

"I'm so glad you're okay," she said in a choked voice. "I was terrified when you were trapped on the other side of the spell with Nicolas."

"You kept telling me there was nothing to worry about," Dante accused.

Serena released me and rolled her eyes. "I was giving

you the support you needed. Had I told you I thought Juliet was in terrible danger, you would have been going crazy with worry, and we never would have gotten anything done."

"We didn't get anything done other than walking the perimeter of the spell and doing some laundry," he pointed out.

Serena flashed him a sweet smile. "The laundry was a very important accomplishment, as was your bath. No matter how much Juliet loves you, she would not have appreciated being subjected to your smell for long."

"I doubt she would have minded," Alaric remarked as he edged closer to Serena. "When we find our mate, we like their natural scent."

"Not always," I argued. "I'm glad Dante bathed."

Dante chuckled. "Then you should thank Serena for pointing out how much I needed it."

"It must be your spellcaster blood," Alaric mused.

"Nope," Elena told him. "We could all use a bath. Everyone here is starting to smell like sweaty, wet dogs."

"That's not true," Alaric argued.

"I'm afraid it is," I chimed in. "When was the last time any of you bathed?"

Though I was certain I could use a bath, it had only been two days since my last one. I'd also cleaned off some after our last fight.

"I agree you should bathe," Sin stated, having changed back to her human form. "It was not pleasant being cooped up in a vehicle with foul-smelling shapeshifters. It's not so much the wet dog smell. I spend a lot of time as a dog, and I rather like wet dogs, but the rest has to go."

"Since we're going to be here for the night, we may as well clean up," Elena suggested.

The others agreed.

Dante pointed to the lake. "It's cold but not too bad. I'll start a fire so you can warm up once you get out."

"A magical fire?" Elena asked. "That was nice and warm."

Dante nodded. "Yes, since we're still trying to conceal our presence here, I'm only using a magical fire unless we need to cook."

After the shapeshifters walked to the lake, Sin hugged Dante.

"I've missed you, warlock."

"Are you back to refusing to use my name?" he asked.

"I'm mad at you," she replied. "You made me worry."

"I hardly think that's my fault," he complained. "You were the one who pushed me in here, or have you forgotten about that?"

Sin looked irritated. "I am tired of all the complaints every time I help people. First, Juliet accused me of intentionally leaving her on the other side. She thought I trapped you inside the Heathergate Refuge to keep her away from you because I don't like her. Now, you're complaining to me, too."

I wasn't sure why the demon suddenly felt overly sensitive, but we were all under a lot of pressure, so I didn't blame her.

"No one is accusing you of anything," I assured her. "I think Dante was a little upset because it sounded like you were saying this situation is his fault."

She released an exasperated huff. "I wasn't blaming him for being trapped, just for making me worry."

"How is that any different?" he asked.

"If all of you would stop making me care about you, then I wouldn't have to worry," she explained as if it was obvious.

"Would it help to know that we were worried about you?" Serena asked.

"Me?" Sin looked between us all as if waiting for someone to explain. "Why would any of you worry about me? I'm a powerful demon—an immortal—not some weak creature who can easily be killed."

"We worry because, even if you are powerful, you could still be harmed," Dante explained. "I'd hate to lose one of my best friends."

Sin blinked twice. "I'm one of your best friends?"

"Mine too," Serena added.

"Same here," I agreed. "You stuck by all of us, and we appreciate it. I hope, even after our adventure, you'll stay with us because I would miss you if you were gone."

"I missed you when you were on the other side of the spell," Dante added.

She looked genuinely touched and a bit annoyed in a way only Sin could pull off.

Chapter Twenty-Five

After setting up for the night, Dante and Serena updated us on all that had happened at the Heathergate Refuge. There wasn't that much to tell. We were all worried about Geori, Fiona, and Darius.

I was even more worried than I'd been when Dante had initially told me, but that had a lot to do with my new fears that my father might have more traitors among his people than I'd first suspected.

Sin had shifted back to dog form, this time taking on one that looked more like a wolf. She was sitting close to Dante as he rubbed her belly.

I no longer felt jealous of their closeness. That could have something to do with the time I'd spent around Sin, or it could simply be that completing the last steps of my bond with Dante made me feel more secure. Either way, I was happy seeing Dante with one of his closest friends by his side.

"If Geori and Fiona met with trouble, then we should spend more time planning before we go looking for Juliet's father," Elena suggested.

Alaric shook his head. "No, that's not an option. Someone is trying to kill Juliet's father. It makes sense to wait here tonight, but I think the risk is too great if we delay any longer."

I was glad Alaric was the one to tell the others we shouldn't wait.

My instincts told me to go in and save my father first thing in the morning. Delaying even this one night made me uneasy, though I knew it was the smartest move. I wasn't convinced that the other shapeshifters would trust my word and move out in the morning, but they respected Alaric and would follow his lead.

"Much as I'd like to spend more time planning, I've had a hard enough time waiting this long," Dante added. "Ellis seemed very worried."

"Yes, Dante and Alaric are right," Serena agreed. "We need to save Juliet's father."

"We'll be in greater danger if we don't save him," I stated. "If Nidia can put Ellis in charge, she'll be the one calling the shots. I'm not sure that even my return will change anything if my father dies. It's a lot harder to remove someone from power."

"I still feel like we need more time to plan, but you all make good points," Elena agreed.

"In the morning, we'll set out," I began. "It will take us about two hours to get to where I believe my father is being held. I'm surprised Fiona wasn't more suspicious of being kept away from my father. There have to be other guards he trusted who betrayed him, or this would never have worked."

"Tell us about the place you think he was taken," Alaric prompted.

"My father has a cabin that only a few close to him know about. It's far from the main community, and he goes there when he needs to get away from it all. It makes the most sense."

"Let's hope he's there," Dante remarked. "I'd rather not have to go into the main community."

"Yes, it would be easier to rescue him from the cabin. I don't think Nidia could post too many guards out there without attracting a lot of attention," I added. "We'll scout around first before anyone makes a move."

"That's a good plan," Alaric agreed. "Now, we should all get some sleep. Who's taking the first watch?"

"No need," Dante replied. "Serena and I set up perimeter spells. We'll know if anyone gets close."

Alaric didn't look convinced. "It's not easy for us to rely on spellcaster magic for our safety."

"Don't you already do that?" I asked. "You must have protection spells in your territory. It's how you were able to find me when I first went looking for you."

"Yes, but those are old," he explained. "I know there's no logic in my argument. It's just that we're used to relying on spells set by long-dead spellcasters."

"We also trust the spell Serena added to protect against the soul eaters," Elena reminded him.

He and the other shapeshifters still looked uneasy.

"Well, you can set up a patrol shift if it makes you feel better," I replied. "It would be best if we all get a good night's sleep."

Alaric nodded. "You're right about us needing rest. I should trust that the protection spell will keep us safe. We'll all try to get some sleep. If we're too edgy, then we'll set up a patrol."

The shapeshifters all went to where they had their beds set up for the night, and Serena looked over at Sin. "You should come sleep by me, Sin. Dante and Juliet need a little time alone."

Sin didn't immediately leave Dante's side, a testament to how much she'd missed him.

"It's okay if you want to stay with us," I assured Sin before looking at Serena. "You're also welcome to stay."

"No, that's okay," Serena replied. "I'm going to sleep closer to the fire."

"You'll be alone," Dante stated.

Sin raised her head to look at Serena and then back at Dante.

"Don't let him make you feel guilty," I told Sin. "Serena doesn't need someone watching over her while she sleeps."

"It would be nice to have someone to cuddle," Serena admitted.

Dante's attention immediately went to Serena. "Are you okay, cousin?"

"I'm fine," she insisted. "Well, I have been worried about Geori."

Dante frowned. "You seemed to be doing fine."

"I've been trying to remain positive since you've been so worried about Juliet."

"When did you start taking care of me?" Dante asked.

I smacked his chest. "You make it sound as if you've been babysitting Serena up until now."

He flashed Serena a sheepish smile. "It did sound that way, and I'm sorry. I'm also sorry I didn't consider what you must be going through. You're very fond of Geori, and we don't know what's going on with him."

Sin stood and made her way over to Serena, obviously deciding that comforting her friend was more important than staying with Dante.

"Do you want to talk?" Dante asked Serena.

She shook her head. "No, I'd like to get some sleep so I'm ready to help Juliet's father tomorrow."

"All right," he agreed. "Goodnight."

"Goodnight," I told Serena and Sin.

"Sleep well," Serena said before turning to walk away with Sin by her side.

Dante sighed. "I've been so caught up in what was going on in my world that I didn't stop to consider Serena's feelings. I have not been a very good cousin."

I rolled my eyes. "Stop it right now. We're not going to sit here and discuss regrets. These have been unusual circumstances. She really has grown closer to Geori, hasn't she?"

"Based on the way she keeps looking at Alaric, I suspect it's nothing more than friendship," he replied.

My gaze moved to where Alaric sat alone. He was watching Serena with an angry scowl. At least, he'd avoided saying anything stupid to her since we'd arrived. That was only because he'd avoided saying more than a few words to Serena, and she'd tried to stay away from him.

It was for the best that they avoided each other. Serena also seemed to realize that, yet I'd still noticed the hurt in her eyes when Alaric hadn't immediately gone to her side after we arrived. Serena might realize that any relationship with Alaric was doomed, but that didn't mean she could simply turn off her feelings for him. It would be so much easier for both of them if that was the case.

"We need to get some sleep," Dante told me, but he made no move to set up our sleeping area.

I was still cuddled up by his side. We were close enough to feel the warmth of the fire, but it was the warmth coming from Dante that kept away the chill. More than the physical chill, it chased away the cold feeling I'd had deep inside while away from him.

"It can't be good to need someone this much," I said with a sigh.

"Why not?" he asked as he looked down at me tucked under his arm.

"I'm willing to change my whole world to be with you," I replied. "What does it say that I'd give up everything for one man?"

"It says that I'm the right man," he replied as he stood and held out a hand to me.

When I took his hand, he helped me to my feet and then led me to the bedroll sitting on the opposite side of the fire from where the shapeshifters were sleeping. He unrolled everything, and I pulled an extra blanket from my bag.

"I can't wait until we can sleep in a bed every night," I mused. "Hopefully, that will be soon."

"No camping in our future?" he asked with a quirked eyebrow.

I looked around and inhaled deeply, savoring the scents of the many trees and plants surrounding us. "Camping sounds good, but only when we want to, and definitely when it's warmer. Even with your magical fire, it's a little chilly."

"Yes, we should wait for a warmer month to camp again," he agreed.

We settled onto the ground, and I rested my head on Dante's chest, sighing as I felt his heart beating under my hand.

"You're mine," I murmured sleepily.

"Always and forever," he agreed.

Chapter Twenty-Six

We only awoke once that night when the protection spell alerted Dante and Serena of an intruder.

I watched a wolf that I immediately recognized as Geori prowl past us. Though I had a lot of questions about what was going on and where Fiona was, it would have to wait until morning. Geori looked exhausted, and his single-minded focus was clear.

He went straight to Serena. With Sin on Serena's left, Geori took up his spot on her right, remaining in wolf form.

"I hope Fiona is okay," I whispered.

"Me too," Dante replied. "Do you want to go over and talk to Geori?"

"No, it can wait a few more hours," I told him. "Geori looked ready to drop."

My hopes of getting answers first thing in the morning were dashed when Alaric woke up first.

"Get away from her!" he roared loud enough to send the flocks of birds by the lake scattering into the sky.

I sat up and looked to where Serena had her bed set up.

Geori was no longer in wolf form, but I didn't know if he had put on shorts since only his bare top half was visible. The same blanket Serena was under covered his lower half.

"Keep your voice down," Serena hissed. "We aren't so isolated here that you can scream at the top of your lungs without worrying about someone hearing you."

Dante and I hurried toward them.

Alaric stood with his hands on his hips as he glared down at Geori. His attention shifted to Dante, and there was no missing the accusation.

"I thought you said there was a protection spell to keep anyone from sneaking up on us," he practically growled and Dante.

"There is, and we saw Geori arrive in the middle of the night," I told Alaric. "He's not an intruder. Geori is on our side."

Alaric's fists clenched and unclenched at his sides as he visibly struggled to get his temper under control. He appeared to be losing that struggle.

"Geori snuck into bed naked with Serena," Alaric growled.

Geori released a frustrated breath before shoving the blanket back to reveal the shorts he wore. He stood and pushed back his dark brown hair as he glared at his friend. His amber eyes were filled with anger. "I joined Serena in wolf form. When I woke up later, I put on shorts. We've been friends our entire lives. Do you think I would try taking advantage of Serena?"

Serena stood and crossed her arms in front of her chest as she glared at Alaric. "Do you think I'm so helpless that I need you to defend me against the advances of my friend? You owe us both an apology."

Alaric looked far from ready to apologize as he continued to glare at Geori. After a long pause, he bit out a grudging apology. "Sorry, I read the situation wrong."

Serena nodded before throwing her arms around Geori. "I'm so glad you're okay. When I saw you show up last night, I was sure I had to be dreaming."

"I'm sorry you were worried," Geori replied as he held her and stroked her hair. "I got back here as soon as I could.”

"We need to know what's going on," I told him. "Today, we plan to go looking for my father, so any information you have may help."

Geori released Serena and nodded. "I didn't see your father. Fiona tried seeing him, but your stepmother wouldn't let her. I'm not sure where he is."

"What about Darius?" I asked.

"Nidia assigned him to guard an ex-council member. He was still trying to locate your father when we got there, but he hasn't had much free time. Nidia is trying to keep all of your father's usual guards too busy to ask questions."

"Where is Fiona?" Dante asked. "I thought she was going to return with you."

"That's what she said at first," Geori agreed. "I don't know if that was ever her plan. When I told her I needed to update you, she said it wasn't her responsibility to update a couple of spellcasters."

"Great," I grumbled.

Fiona's attitude irritated me, though it didn't surprise me. She might have been willing to put up with Dante and Serena's input to some extent because they'd helped me, but in the end, her loyalty was to the Heathergate Refuge. If she didn't believe Dante and Serena could help with the current threat, they were of no use to her.

I was still grateful that she hadn't sent guards after them.

"Did she give you any messages for us?" Dante asked.

"No, but I didn't tell her I was leaving," Geori admitted.

"You were worried she'd try stopping you," I deduced.

He nodded. "Yes, she seemed to like having me there as an ally, and she wanted me to help her find your father. I couldn't leave my friends out here with no back-up."

Dante quirked an eyebrow. "Your friends? I got the impression you weren't overly fond of me."

"Geori gives everyone that impression," Elena stated. "I've known him since we were children, and I'm not always sure he likes me."

"I know Geori's my friend," Serena argued. "I knew before he said anything. You don't understand him."

"And how did you become such an expert on Geori?" Alaric demanded.

"Knock it off," Serena hissed. "We need to focus on saving Juliet's father. You will act like a reasonable male, and you will remember that Geori is one of your best friends."

Alaric blew out a frustrated breath. "It makes me crazy seeing him close to you."

"You don't have any right to act jealous," Serena told him before looking at Geori. "Do you have any information that will help us?"

"Not much," he admitted. "Juliet's stepmother is always surrounded by the same guards. There are fifteen, and they're the only ones she seems to trust. She claims Juliet's father is fine but needs time alone to grieve."

"We saw Juliet's brother, Ellis, while you were away, and he told us his father is very sick," Dante added. "It sounds like poison. He also told us his father's illness is supposed to be a secret."

Geori nodded. "I didn't talk to Ellis, but he seems upset. Fiona thought it could be that he's bothered by the prospect of being the future leader. He was rude to her the only time we got close to him."

"What was the reaction to the perimeter spell being locked?" Serena asked. "I'm surprised there haven't been more shapeshifters patrolling the edge to try and figure out what's going on."

"Nidia told Fiona to keep that information to herself," Geori replied. "All trips to the trading post were canceled before that happened because several spellcasters were spotted near the Heathergate Refuge. I'm not clear on when that happened."

"Someone probably saw Nicolas and the other spellcasters he had out here hunting us," I mused. "It works out well for Nidia that no one can leave the

Heathergate Refuge."

"How so?" Dante asked. "It seems this could backfire if they need supplies."

I shook my head. "We don't *need* any of the items we get at the trading post. They're luxuries. The bracelets might be considered a necessity, but they're only important for those of us who need to leave the Heathergate Refuge. She can delay getting those for the babies or those who've broken their bracelets. Sometimes, there are messages from the trading posts sent directly for my father, and it would look suspicious if she blocked too many of those, so keeping everyone away from there is helping her keep his illness hidden."

"If she had to admit to his illness, more healers would likely get involved," Dante remarked. "He's the leader, so there are those who would want to make sure every effort was being made."

"True," I agreed. "I'm sure she has a healer seeing him, but one loyal to her."

"A killer," Serena said angrily. "Someone is helping her hide his illness and probably pretending to treat him."

"That healer will back up her story later and claim to have done everything to try and save my father. Nidia has probably come up with some great excuse for keeping his condition a secret, likely something to do with fears it would cause more problems so soon after my death. She's a very good liar."

"What did Fiona say to get you close to Nidia?" I asked.

"Fiona said I was from one of the outlying families that often helped with perimeter guard duty," Geori explained. "Nidia dismissed me as insignificant. She's very cold. I'm not sure anyone will expect her to show much emotion regarding her mate's illness."

"Geori is right," I agreed. "Nidia is even cold with Ellis, but I know she loves him. Does Fiona have any idea which of my father's guards we can still trust?"

"Fiona says Nidia sent several of them on long tours as

perimeter guards," Geori replied. "According to Fiona, a few must have been trapped outside, but nearly all of them returned."

I smiled. "That must be driving Nidia crazy. She can't keep my father hidden from them for too much longer."

"Unless there are more traitors than Fiona suspects."

I frowned because Dante was right.

How many of the guards closest to my father were working with Nidia?

We already knew there had to be at least a few of them in order to pull this off. My stepmother wouldn't have been able to reassign all of his inner circle guards without causing too much suspicion. It was a given that any assigned to guard him after he got sick were traitors, and it seemed likely that those assigned to perimeter guard duty were loyal to him.

"It would help if I could get more information from Fiona," I remarked. "Then, I might have a better idea of who I can trust."

"I say we trust no one for now," Serena replied. "We stick to the first part of the plan and find your father. After he's safe, then we can decide who to trust."

Dante nodded. "That's the best plan."

"Do you know where he is?" Geori asked.

"I'm pretty sure," I replied. "If he's not at the first place, then I have some other ideas."

"Maybe we should scout the areas where you think he might be first," Alaric suggested. "It will be easier for us to get around in wolf form, and we're less likely to be recognized."

"No, I think that's a bad idea," I replied. "We have a large mix of animal forms here, whereas you all seem to change into wolves."

Geori nodded his agreement. "This is one place where I think we'll be less noticeable in human form."

I wondered why so many of the rebel shapeshifters were wolves in their animal form. It seemed like a strange coincidence, though it could be just that.

I shook off those thoughts. There was no time to worry about that now; we needed to find my father.

"Okay, we should all eat and get moving," I told the others. "Some of us should move the car closer to the cabin we're checking first. I know a spot where we can keep it hidden. We may need the supplies in there."

"All right," Dante agreed. "Let's get ready to head out."

Chapter Twenty-Seven

I'd been fairly confident that we'd find my father at his old retreat, but he wasn't there. I was standing in the kitchen, looking around for any signs he might have been there recently, but I found none.

"Don't worry," Dante said as he slipped an arm around my shoulders and pulled me close. "We still have other places to check."

I nodded and forced a smile. "You're right. It's always possible Nidia doesn't know about this place. I don't recall him ever bringing her here."

"That could be very good for us," Serena remarked. "If it's unlikely anyone will stop by, we can set up base here and stop carrying so much of our gear everywhere we go. There's also a shower. I'd prefer to avoid jumping in the cold lake again."

"Good point," I agreed. "It doesn't look like anyone has been here in months."

"And we can bring your father back here once we find him," Alaric added. "He'll need time to recover."

"He definitely will if he's been given any kind of poison for very long," Dante agreed.

"All right," I replied. "Let's stash some of our stuff here and then head to the next stop."

I had everyone hide their gear in case someone stopped by to check the cabin. Even someone loyal to my father would sound the alarm if they thought intruders were using his getaway.

The cabin was large enough to comfortably hold all of us that night. My father had it built so he could take me there as a child. It was our special place, and I had my own room. There were two other bedrooms for guards, one for my father, and one for Ellis that had never been used as far as I knew.

My father always talked about the three of us going there, but I'd argued against sharing my special time with my father. Now, I felt selfish for having excluded my brother.

"When you mentioned a hidden cabin, I pictured something smaller," Serena said as we walked away from the cabin.

"Same here," Alaric agreed. "This isn't something you could hide."

"There's no need to hide the outlying homes," I explained. "Those that live in them are the members of the Heathergate Refuge who want to be left alone, and we respect their wishes. Rules against bothering any of the outlying families were put in place before my father built his cabin."

"It must be nice to get away sometimes," Elena mused. "I imagine it's peaceful to have a place where you can be alone."

"Since when do you feel the need to be alone?" Alaric asked. "Geori is moody and antisocial, so I'd expect him to say something like that, but not you."

Serena frowned. "Geori isn't antisocial. He's selectively social."

Geori laughed. "Selectively social. I like that."

"Very selective," Elena said under her breath.

"That's not a bad thing," Dante pointed out. "There are a lot of people who aren't worth your time. I didn't exactly have an active social life in Azuredale."

"Except for the many witches Serena said you used to bring back to your room," I teased.

"How many witches?" Geori asked.

"I did not bring a constant string of witches back to my room," Dante argued.

"But you did bring some," Alaric pushed.

Dante glared at him. "Are you trying to get me in trouble with Juliet?"

"She's the one who brought it up," Alaric reminded him.

"In jest," I pointed out. "Serena was messing with him at the time."

"So you brought no witches to your room?"

Serena glared at Geori.

"What?" Geori asked.

"I'm starting to regret bringing this up," I admitted.

"Because you're worried that having Dante admit the truth of his past exploits will change how you feel about him?" Alaric asked.

"Past exploits?" Dante asked with a bark of laughter.

"So, there were no witches?" Elena asked.

"There were witches, but not as many as I implied," Serena explained. "Can we let this go before Juliet regrets teasing Dante and starts feeling jealous?"

"When I first met Sin, I was jealous of her relationship with Dante," I admitted. "I was even a little jealous of the witches from Dante's past."

"And now?" Dante asked, sounding worried about my response.

"Not now," I replied honestly. "It's strange, but since that last piece of our magical bond fell into place, I don't feel an ounce of jealousy. We're connected, and I know your heart is mine. I know you'd never stray."

"I think that's how shapeshifters feel once they find their mate," Elena replied.

"Only after they accept their mate," I reminded her, my gaze moving to Alaric. "Before they accept their mate, a male shapeshifter acts a lot like Alaric around Serena."

"Alaric is in a mood for other reasons," Geori replied for him. "This is a stressful time."

"Yes, it's stressful for us all," Serena agreed. "I've never met any spellcasters who've bound their magic, but this is supposed to be how they feel."

"Why do so few spellcasters bind their magic?" I asked. "Is it just that few find someone with compatible magic."

"It's all about trust and control," Dante replied. "In order to bind their magic, two spellcasters must give away a piece of their own power. It feels more like we share parts of our magic, not that one took power from the other."

"I wonder if those who do bind their magic are stronger," Alaric mused. "It makes a shapeshifter more powerful to take a mate, and it seems that being able to share magic would make both spellcasters stronger."

"It does in some cases but not all," Dante replied. "There is a certain amount of risk involved. Many are afraid it will weaken them."

"Some spellcasters also fear the emotional connection," Serena added. "There isn't a telepathic link, but there is a certain empathic connection. They can't hide their feelings."

Dante nodded. "That's true."

"We have that, too," I replied. "I think that's part of the reason I'm not worried about Dante straying. I have no doubts about his feelings for me. I'm glad we're bound, but I'm not sure how it happened."

"It's not like shapeshifter or spellcaster bindings, which require both sides to agree," Dante added. "This just sort of happened."

"I'm not sure that's completely true," I argued. "We could have fought it."

Dante considered what I'd said. "You're probably right. I never considered the possibility of resisting when our magic joined."

"Neither did I," I agreed. "I couldn't even put two thoughts together. I'm glad it happened in phases, or it might have turned my brain to mush. It was very intense."

"It sounds terrifying," Alaric replied.

"Yes, I'm not sure I'd like it," Elena agreed.

Geori was looking at Serena when he spoke. "It could be amazing with the right person. I've often felt lonely, and it would be nice having someone I love truly understand me."

"Yes, it would," Serena agreed.

Chapter Twenty-Eight

The next outlying cabin belonged to a couple I didn't know all that well, though I'd visited them with my father several times.

They had always been quiet and standoffish. I got the impression they were annoyed with my father for bringing me with him when he visited. My father claimed they were loyal allies he would trust with his life, but he'd also trusted the guards who'd left me in an Azurean trap.

I didn't believe anyone other than my father ever visited them. It would be a good place to hide him, though my gut told me they weren't traitors.

"We're nearly there," I told the others. "I think this might be a good place for some of you to shift into wolves and scout around the back of the property to see if there are guards."

"Agreed," Alaric replied before motioning for two shapeshifters to follow him.

They returned about fifteen minutes later.

"It doesn't look like anyone is guarding the cabin," Alaric said as he dressed.

"Do you think it's worth checking places with no guards?" Serena asked. "I'd think that if your father was being held there, they'd have guards posted around the outside. There probably wouldn't be a lot, but at least a few. That's what I've been thinking since we checked your father's secret getaway."

"You're probably right, but it will bother me if I don't see for myself. There's also a chance this couple might be able to help us. My father trusted them."

"Just because they aren't hiding your father doesn't mean they aren't traitors," Alaric pointed out.

"I know," I agreed. "I just think they aren't, and I know that sounds crazy when I said they might be holding my father there."

"Let's go with your instincts on this one," Dante replied. "We need more back-up, so we're going to have to trust someone eventually."

"It would be best if only a couple of us go to the door so it doesn't look like we're here to start a fight. The rest of you can stay close by in case there's trouble."

"I'll go with you," Serena offered.

"No, I will," Dante insisted.

"I'm the least threatening in appearance," Serena reminded him. "Sin can come with us. They won't expect a dog to be a problem unless there are shapeshifters who turn into dogs." She looked at Geori. "Are there?"

"No, but it would be best if the demon changed into a dog who looks less like a wolf," he suggested.

The air around Sin vibrated and turned hazy as she transformed into a very small dog, even smaller than my cat form.

Serena grinned. "That's perfect."

Tension vibrated through me as we walked up to the front door of the cabin. No one rushed out to attack us, but I still had no way of knowing how the couple would react to my presence.

Would we be attacked?

Would guards be waiting for us?

Would the sight of me still alive be too much for the elderly couple living there to take?

These were all things I worried about, but nothing

could have prepared me for what happened as I was about to knock on the front door.

Before my fist connected with the wood, the door flew open, and I came face to face with my brother. At nine, Ellis was only a few inches shorter than me.

His brown eyes were wide with shock as he stared at me.

He looked at Serena and then back at me as if not quite believing his eyes.

"You found my sister!" he said to Serena with genuine joy. "It is you, isn't it, Juliet?"

"Yes, Ellis," I replied. "I'm back."

Ellis threw his arms around me and wept. "I thought you were gone forever. My mother said you were dead. She said she saw your body, and I was so mean to you the last time I saw you. I'm sorry."

"Mean to me?" I asked, not recalling the occasion.

He pulled away slightly and wiped his tears as he tried to compose himself. "I told you I wished I'd never had a sister, but I didn't mean it. I was mad because you told my mother about me sneaking off to the lake with my friends when I was supposed to be doing lessons."

I frowned. "I never told your mother about you sneaking off to the lake. This is the first I'm hearing about you skipping lessons." I waved off those concerns. "None of that matters now. I don't remember you saying that to me, and I'm not mad at you. You don't have to apologize."

"I do," he whispered. "It was so awful thinking you died believing I hate you. It was worse because I never got to know you."

"I never thought you hated me, and now we have a chance to get to know each other," I assured him. "Where are Case and Brea?"

"Right here," Case said as he stepped forward.

His hair had been gray and his skin wrinkled my entire life.

"Why is Ellis here?" I asked, suddenly feeling very suspicious of my brother's presence at Case and Brea's home.

"You should come in before someone sees you," Case announced.

"Am I safe here?" I asked.

Case looked annoyed. "Irritating girl! Showing up at my door and then acting like I'd hurt you. That's nerve for you."

"I have good reason for being paranoid after all I've been through," I told him. "Can some of my friends come in with me?"

He shrugged and stepped back. "Suit yourself, but it might be smart to leave some guards outside. I imagine you're in a lot of trouble."

"That's an understatement," I agreed.

"What kind of trouble?" Ellis asked.

I felt sadness wash over me as I looked at my brother. There was no way this could end happily for him.

"It might be best if I talk to Case and Brea alone," I told Ellis.

His eyes narrowed. "Whatever happened to you affects me and everyone else at the Heathergate Refuge. I will not be sent away like some dumb kid who needs to be protected. These are my people, and you are my sister. I already know this has something to do with my mother, and I can deal with that."

My father and I had been very much mistaken about Ellis. He might not be ready to take over as leader yet, but he had what it took.

I decided to bring Dante, Serena, Sin in her small dog form, and Geori in with us. Though it was clearly a struggle, Alaric held his tongue and waited outside.

After introductions, I told Case, Brea, and Ellis all that had happened since I'd left for the trading post. No one spoke right after I finished.

Case looked thoughtful.

Brea looked horrified.

Ellis looked furious.

"We need to figure out where my father is and try to

counteract the poison he's been given," I explained.

"And you thought we might be holding your father hostage here?" Case demanded.

I shrugged. "I thought it was a possibility. My father always trusted you, but I don't know you all that well. I'm not willing to put my faith in anyone who hasn't proven they deserve my trust."

Case nodded. "Fair enough. I never did get to know you or your brother all that well. To be honest, I was shocked when Ellis started showing up here every day or so."

"I didn't think anyone would look for me here," Ellis explained.

"You poor boy," Serena crooned. "This has been awful for you."

"It's better now that I have my sister back," he whispered.

"I'm sorry I had to give you news like this about your mother," I told him.

He shrugged. "She's never been all that nice to me either. Lately, she's been angry because I don't want to become the leader. I just want our father back."

I had always seen my brother as pampered and believed my stepmother gave him everything he wanted, but it seemed her lies had fooled me. She treated Ellis differently when I wasn't watching.

In truth, I'd avoided spending time around either of them for years, preferring to steer clear of the inevitable drama that would upset my father.

I shook off those thoughts. Later, after we rescued my father, I could worry about my relationship with my brother. I could also start worrying about any damage his mother might have done to him.

My attention moved to Case and Brea. "We have some ideas of places to check, but do you have any suggestions?"

Brea nodded. "I think he's at the old healer's cottage near the west end of the Heathergate Refuge. It's the one right by the falls."

Case considered her suggestion before nodding. "I think you're right. If anyone starts looking for him and realizes he's sick, it will be easy to explain his presence there. I don't trust that old hag."

"Neither do I," Brea agreed. "She was never all that great of a healer if you ask me."

"Old hag?" I asked. "I thought you were talking about Magda."

"I am," Brea replied. "I stand by my description."

"Magda is my father's age," I remarked. "Everyone was surprised when she moved to one of the outer cabins since she's so young."

"I'm surprised she wasn't ordered to move out there earlier," Brea stated.

Case nodded. "Your father put up with her attitude for longer than I would have. She hated your mother and used to say horrible things about you. I'd retired from my duties as a guard by then, and even I heard some of the gossip she spread."

"She didn't like my mother?" I asked.

"I don't think it was a matter of her disliking your mother so much as jealousy," Brea clarified. "She always expected your father to take her as his mate. After he made his choice, she started spreading ugly rumors about your mother. Magda didn't believe your mother was from one of the outlying families and called her an outsider who'd usurped her place as your father's mate. Your father got Magda to behave for a long time, but then she started in with her lies again when you were older, so he told her she could either leave the Heathergate Refuge or retire to an isolated cabin."

"Nidia would know about her anger toward my father," I mused. "Magda sounds like someone who'd be willing to help, as long as she wasn't jealous of Nidia."

"I think that although she is jealous, she might still be willing to side with your stepmother," Serena remarked. "She had no chance with your father by the time Nidia came into the picture, and she's likely looking for revenge."

Case nodded. "I doubt she's let go of her grudge against your father."

"We should update the others outside and then go to Magda's. Even if my father isn't at her place, she may still know where he is," I stated.

"I'm going with you," my brother announced.

"Absolutely not," I replied.

"Why not?" he demanded. "He's my father, too, and he's in danger. I'm not weak, especially not when I'm in my animal form."

"No, I'm not letting you put yourself in danger. It's out of the question."

Chapter Twenty-Nine

No matter how hard I argued that he couldn't go, Ellis refused to listen. It was either bring him with us in the car or let him travel there on his own. I decided it would be easier to keep him safe if he stayed with us.

Case and Brea had gotten us another vehicle so we could travel faster. They'd both stayed behind so Case could rally those he knew were loyal to my father. I was surprised to find that he still had contact with quite a few members of my father's old guard when he seemed like such a recluse.

I sat in the front seat with Sin on my lap, still in the form of a small dog. Serena, Ellis, and Elena were in the backseat. Dante was driving. Alaric and Geori had argued that one of them should ride with Serena, but I wanted to avoid shapeshifter drama.

"You don't seem like spellcasters," Ellis remarked.

"Have you met any other spellcasters?" I asked him.

"Maybe," Ellis replied. "I didn't know these two were spellcasters, so maybe I've met a lot of them and just didn't know it."

"I don't think we have any other spellcasters here at the Heathergate Refuge," I replied. "I was surprised by the similarities between shapeshifters and spellcasters myself."

We weren't sharing the details of my mixed heritage with anyone yet. Once we rescued my father, I was more than willing to relinquish my role as future leader in order to keep the peace among my people, but first, we had to rescue my father. It wasn't the right time to add more potential issues.

"Do you think maybe spellcasters aren't all that dangerous?" Ellis asked.

"No," Serena replied. "They are very dangerous. Some of us are not your enemy, but there are plenty who are. It's best to assume they're all a threat unless your sister tells you otherwise."

"I can trust you, right?" Ellis asked Serena.

"Yes, you can trust me," she assured him.

"Serena saved my life," I told him. "So did Dante."

"And Dante is your mate," he added. "I can't wait to tell my friends about this."

"I'm not sure they'll be as excited with the news as you are," I warned him.

"Why not?" he asked. "They were worried because I've been sad since I thought you died. They'll be happy you're alive, and they already like Dante and Serena. They'll like them even more once I tell them Dante and Serena saved your life."

"Hopefully, more than you and your friends will feel that way," I replied.

"Are you going to leave again?" Ellis asked.

"Maybe," I admitted. "I need to stay with Dante and Serena, and I'm not sure they'll be allowed to live here."

"It seems unlikely," Serena added.

"Not that we would blame your people for wanting us to leave," Dante stated.

"You have to stay here," Ellis argued. "You're the future leader."

"They'll still have you," I reminded him.

He snorted. "I don't think so. Being in charge sounds awful."

I smiled. "Yeah, I felt the same. In fact, I'm still not

sure I like the idea, but it's growing on me. When I was your age, I fought against being the future ruler."

"I'd make a terrible leader," Ellis argued. "I don't know the first thing about being in charge of our people. Father says I don't have the temperature."

I smiled. "Temperament. It basically means that your personality isn't right for the job, but I disagree. Even if I stay, I may not be able to take my place as our father's heir. You still need to be prepared. If there's one thing this time should teach us, it's that we never know if something will happen to me."

"All right," he agreed. "I guess I need to prepare in case something happens to you before you have kids to take over."

"And you need to be prepared for the fact that my children may not be accepted because they'll be part-spellcaster," I pointed out. "For what it's worth, I think you'd make a good leader when you grow up."

"I don't, but it makes me feel better that you think I would," he replied.

We parked about a mile from the cabin, hoping to sneak up to the house without alerting any guards. One benefit of dealing with shapeshifters over demons and spellcasters was that there were no perimeter spells around the cabin.

My unease about having Ellis with us grew after we parked and prepared for the hike. I didn't want him to get hurt. He'd decided to remain in human form, leaving him more vulnerable. At least, he'd dressed in shorts and a t-shirt so he could quickly strip down and change into a bear if needed.

"This is so exciting," Sin announced, having suddenly changed to her human form. This time, she was dressed in leather pants, a leather bustier, and black boots.

"Where did she come from?" Ellis asked as he took several steps back.

I didn't blame him for sounding nervous. Sin didn't look human with her red eyes.

"This is my friend, Sin," I explained. "She's also able to shapeshift."

"What is she?" he asked as he moved a step closer to study her.

"A demon," Sin replied.

Ellis's eyes widened, and while he still looked afraid, fear was giving way to fascination. "I didn't even know demons were real. Are you going to live with us, too?"

Sin shrugged. "I'll probably stick around if my friends stay—for now, anyway. They could get into all sorts of trouble without me."

"You've gotten us out of a lot of trouble," I agreed.

"You were the dog," Ellis remarked as he moved closer. "You have the same energy. I thought your energy felt off."

Sin grinned and looked at me. "I like your brother. He's smart."

"Yes, he is," I agreed. "We need to start moving, so we should also try to keep the chatter down and pay attention to our surroundings."

Sin frowned. "But I just changed to this form. I haven't been able to talk for hours."

"You may get to kill someone," Dante remarked.

That seemed to brighten Sin's mood. "Then we should get moving. After we kill your enemy, I want to get to know Ellis better."

She skipped ahead, and no one tried stopping her. Sin could handle any guards she ran into.

My focus remained on keeping my brother safe. I didn't believe Nidia was evil enough to kill her own child, but I wouldn't want to bet Ellis's life on that belief.

We didn't run into any guards patrolling the surrounding area, but there were six outside when we got close to the cabin. This had to be where my father was being kept. I also recognized two of the guards as the ones who'd been with Nidia the day she'd taken my bracelet.

Alaric and his shapeshifters all changed to wolf form for the fight, and Ellis changed to his bear form. Sin shifted to the form of a small dog and took her place at my side. Dante was on my other side, and I could feel him gathering magic.

"Where is my father?" I demanded of the two traitors standing guard in front of the house.

Their eyes widened, and they both stared for several heartbeats.

"You look shocked to see me," I said with a pleasant smile.

"It can't be," one whispered. "This has to be some kind of trick."

"Who are you?" the other demanded.

"You know who I am," I told them. "You were there when I was put in that trap. Did you hope I'd die quickly or be enslaved as the life was drained from me?"

One looked defiant while the other looked afraid.

The defiant guard spoke first. "Foolish girl! You should have stayed hidden. Do you really think there are enough still loyal to your father to keep you alive? We all know the truth about what you are. Your father deserves to die for trying to pass you off as our leader."

The fearful guard looked between us as if trying to decide which was the greater threat. "I wasn't trying to kill you, Juliet. You have to understand that we cannot let someone with mixed blood become the ruler of the Heathergate Refuge. It's not natural. Your father shouldn't have lied to us."

The other guard's face flushed with anger as he bit out his next words. "You don't have to suck up to her. She's a weak shapeshifter and no threat to us."

"Idiots," Dante said with a laugh. "First, Juliet is far from weak. Second, she has very powerful friends. I suggest you take us to her father, or we'll kill you."

The guard looked less defiant when he replied. "Do you think it's just us here? You're outnumbered."

"Stupid mortals," Sin taunted as she shifted to her human form.

Dante smiled. "You don't have to die here today. You

can surrender and live."

"Please, don't surrender," Sin purred as she stalked closer.

The defiant guard drew a knife and lunged at her, but Dante was faster, hitting the hand holding the blade with a blast of magic.

Sin frowned at Dante. "You said I could play with them."

"Only after we handle business," Dante reminded her before looking at the other guard. "And you can only play with the ones who don't cooperate."

Hearing the commotion, the other guards raced around the sides of the house. I didn't need to look behind me to know the shapeshifters and Serena were already approaching. The guards who'd come to help took tentative steps back as they watched with wide eyes. Their eyes moved from me to my approaching back-up.

"Where is my father?" I demanded.

"You're too late," the defiant guard taunted, still clutching his injured hand. "Your father will be dead soon, and you'll join him."

"Now, it's time to play," Sin cooed as she continued toward him.

The guards sprang into action, realizing they only had two choices—fight or die.

Chapter Thirty

The guards rushed us as our back-up moved forward to deal with them.

A guard took one wolf down with a tranquilizer dart before another sank his teeth into the hand holding the dart gun.

Serena focused on using her magic to keep the guards from getting too close to where she and Ellis stood while Dante and I fought our way into the house. Once we burst through the front door, Magda jumped out and tossed a black orb—a death spell—at us. I shoved Dante out of the way in time, and the orb hit the wall.

As Magda reached toward her pocket, I spun and kicked her arm. I needed to keep her distracted while Dante went to find my father. Some of the healing spells Calista had given us were powders and needed spellcaster magic to activate them.

"You're an abomination, just like your mother!" she shouted.

"Poor Magda," I taunted. "My father turned you down in favor of another female twice. He picked my mother over you, and then he picked Nidia. It must hurt being so unwanted."

She shrieked and lunged at me with her fingers curled

into claws as if she might tear out my throat.

Magda's greatest weakness seemed to be her temper; it made her careless.

I ducked before she reached me and shoved her into a nearby table. She managed to stay on her feet. Grabbing the chair, she tossed it at me. I avoided being hit in the face, but it still slammed into my shoulder.

"You and your father will die!" Magda shouted as she grabbed another chair.

I was faster and tossed a glass vase at her head. It hit her in the forehead and shattered.

Magda stumbled back and wiped the blood from her face. Before she could recover and attack again, I landed a side kick that knocked her to the ground. When she started to stand, I kicked her in the chin, and she fell back. This time, she didn't get up.

I secured her arms and legs, wincing at the pain in my shoulder.

Once she was tied up, I hurried toward the back of the cabin, where I could hear Dante saying the words to a spell.

I ran into the room, worried he wouldn't find the right spell to save my father.

Dante's hands were just above my father's bare chest, and I could see the way my father struggled for each breath. He'd lost a lot of weight, and his skin was like greenish-gray paper wrapped around his bones.

It was enough to make me gasp as I dropped to my knees beside the bed he was lying on.

"Father," I whispered. "Please, don't die."

"Juliet." His voice was ragged and weak. When his eyes opened, they were glazed. "I must be dead. Where is your mother? Now, we can all be together again."

"I'm not dead, and neither are you," I assured him. "We're going to make you better."

"How is this even possible? Nidia saw your body. The rogue shapeshifters killed you." He closed his eyes and released a shuddering breath. "I'm hallucinating again. I see you often, but the male with you is new."

"This is Dante. He's my mate," I explained. "He saved me and brought me back to you."

"Back in my dreams." He let out another shuddering breath.

"I think this one is working," Dante said in a soft voice. "The first three spells I tried had no effect on his condition, but he's finally breathing easier. We made it just in time."

I swallowed hard as I looked down at my father. "Do you think he'll recover? He looks near death."

"I don't know," Dante admitted. "It will help if we can get a healer you trust to look at him."

I nodded and swallowed back my pain at seeing my father so frail.

I would not let the people who'd betrayed and tried to kill my father go unpunished. It was time to move on to the next phase of our plan.

Standing, I took a deep, calming breath. "We need to move him to another location."

Dante nodded. "I agree. Who knows how long we have before someone shows up here? They likely have other guards taking shifts, and your stepmother will want updates."

"Nidia will show up here to find out how my father is doing," I agreed. "To pull off her story about being the grieving mate, she'll want to show others that she visited my father often while he was sick."

"Are we still taking him back to his cabin?" Dante asked.

"I think Case and Brea's place is a better idea," I replied. "Brea has some healing experience. My father told me that it came from patching up Case so often. I don't know how much she'll be able to do in this situation, but at least she can keep an eye on him."

"It might be best if we convince Serena to stay by his side in case he needs more magical intervention," Dante replied.

"Good thinking," I agreed. "Let's go see if we have any prisoners to deal with, and then we can move my father."

Chapter Thirty-One

Case had gathered twenty shapeshifters he believed to be completely loyal to my father. Several were older or from outlying families. It seemed many living away from the main community were grateful to my father for mostly leaving them alone. They were loyal to him and didn't seem fond of Nidia.

We'd just gotten my father settled into a room, and Brea was still with him.

The plan to leave Serena behind with my father hadn't been brought up yet. I was hoping he'd be doing much better before we had to make a decision. So far, it looked as if we might not need to leave Serena behind to help Brea.

I stood outside of Case and Brea's home with all but Brea and Ellis.

"I want to avoid as many casualties as possible," I began as I addressed the others. "We need to get my stepmother away from the main community."

"She'll check on your father, so you could wait for her at Magda's," Case suggested.

"That seems like a good plan," Serena agreed.

"Unless she's already gone there and realized your father is missing," Dante added. "In that case, we could waste a lot of time. The guards we captured said she'd notice they were missing soon. They could have been lying, but I think we should still try to find another place to lure her."

I nodded. "I agree.

"I have an idea," Ellis announced.

I hadn't realized he'd returned from sitting with our father.

"What do you think we should do?" I asked.

"I should go back and tell my mother I saw you with some rogue shapeshifters," he explained.

"Will she believe you?" I asked.

"Probably not if I'm the only one who saw you," he admitted. "I can always get some of my friends to say they were with me. My mom thinks I'm staying at my friend, Jaden's, while my teacher is taking a break to help his mate with their new cub, so she'll believe I was out with my friends."

"And Jaden will back up your story?" I asked.

"I don't have a friend named Jaden," Ellis admitted. "My mother doesn't know much about any of my friends."

"That's an excellent idea," Dante agreed. "If Nidia thinks she may be able to take Juliet and her allies by surprise, she won't delay in heading out to confront them."

"True," I began. "Nidia will want to make sure no one else sees me alive or hears about her betrayal. Her fear of having anyone else talk to me will make her act more rashly."

Ellis grinned. "We make a good team."

I hugged him. "Yes, we do. This seems like a good plan. First, we need to decide who's going to stay here with our father, and then we need to figure out the best place for this confrontation."

"I'll stay behind if it looks like your father needs a spellcaster to help with his recovery," Serena offered. "I'd rather fight with you, so I hope it won't come to that, but we should have a plan just in case."

"We really could use another spellcaster," Sin mused. "When can we leave? I'm ready for another fight."

"We need to finish planning," I reminded her.

Sin let out a dramatic sigh. "I hate planning. It's so boring."

"I think you should go with Ellis, Sin," Serena suggested.

"Why?" Sin asked. "He won't be in much danger, and it's less likely I'll get to kill anyone."

"It would make me feel better if you were with Ellis, but I don't think it would work," I added. "You wouldn't be able to get near Nidia in any of the forms I've seen you use."

Ellis nodded. "My mother hates dogs, and she would never let one get anywhere near her. I can't think of any shape that Sin could take to get close to my mother. If she knows our father is missing, she'll be suspicious of every adult. What she's been doing will get her killed."

I placed a hand on my brother's shoulder. "Are you sure you want to be involved with luring your mother into a trap? I know you feel like this is the right thing to do, but I don't want to see you hurt or suffering any guilt later. She's your mother, and I know you love her."

He shrugged. "I guess I love her, and maybe I will feel a little bad later. Not so much as you think. Every time she tells me I'm useless and weak, I wish she'd leave and never come back. I only have friends because I used to sneak off to play with the other kids. That always got me in trouble, just like when I used to want to spend time with you. She's only letting me stay with a friend now because she doesn't want me around while I don't have lessons."

"Why didn't you tell your father?" Serena asked.

"She made me feel like it was my fault," he admitted. "I tried telling my father once, but I ended up saying I made it up after my mother said I was lying like Juliet."

I felt raw fury building inside of me. After the abuse I'd suffered at the hands of my stepmother, I had good reason to hate her even before her betrayal. Finding out she'd also been abusing my brother made me furious.

It wasn't just Nidia who I was furious with; I also felt

anger at my father for ignoring a problem that was right in front of his face. I shook off that anger. Later, I would confront my father after he recovered and we'd dealt with Nidia.

"I'm sorry I didn't help you," I told Ellis.

"We'll help each other now, right?" Ellis asked.

I nodded and hoped I wasn't lying to my brother since I still didn't know if I could stay at the Heathergate Refuge.

"Are you sure you can do this?" I asked. "We can find another way to draw her out."

"I can do it," he promised. "I need to find my friends, and you'll have to let me go alone, or it will look suspicious."

That part of the plan made me most uneasy. "There has to be another way."

"I should be able to get away with walking Ellis back there," Case stated. "No one will think anything of me complaining that he was in some kind of trouble. I'm known for being antisocial and angry. I can also get away with hanging around in case he needs help."

"Does Nidia know you still see my father?" I asked.

Case shrugged. "She's never come out this way with him. The last time I saw her was when I'd gone for supplies. I got into a heated argument with your father that day. We do that often."

"Can you get away with backing Ellis on his story about seeing Juliet?" Dante asked. "That seems like a better plan than involving more children."

Case hesitated. "That would mean drawing Nidia to my place. This isn't the best place for a confrontation."

"You can say you saved me from drowning in the lake," Ellis suggested.

"You learned to swim after you almost drowned," I argued.

Ellis shook his head. "I can only swim in bear form. Father said he'd get me lessons, but I haven't had them yet."

"That could work, then," I mused. "The lake is a good

spot for a fight since no one can sneak up on us from behind."

"Then we have a plan!" Ellis said excitedly.

"We have the beginnings of a plan," Case corrected him. "It's definitely a good start."

Chapter Thirty-Two

We continued working on our plans until after sunset. Ellis seemed annoyed that we needed to wait another day, but it was too late to make a move.

None of us felt comfortable camping when there might be shapeshifters out looking for my father, but we had no other options. There were too many of us to sleep in Case and Brea's place.

We'd discussed some of us going back to my father's cabin but ended up deciding against splitting our fighters.

Our next big argument came when setting up a patrol schedule for the night. Though we'd all be fighting on the same side in the morning, the rebel shapeshifters didn't trust those from the Heathergate Refuge, and that distrust was mutual. Each set up their own patrols for the night.

Ellis and Serena were staying in the room with my father in case he needed more help. He had only woken up for a short time since we'd moved him, but it seemed like a good sign that Brea had been able to get him to drink some broth.

After Dante and I finished handling the first patrol shift, we set up our bedroll close to the cabin.

"I hate waiting as much as Ellis," I grumbled as I laid down beside Dante. "I know it's the smart thing to do, but I really want this over."

Dante rolled to his side to face me. "I know how you feel. Waiting is always the worst. It looks like we should be able to bring Serena with us. Your father likely won't need a spellcaster to stay with him."

"It would be nice to have another spellcaster in the fight," I agreed. "Do you really think my father is doing better? I'm worried because he's still sleeping so much."

"He's doing much better," Dante assured me. "Get some sleep, my impatient little cat."

I smacked his chest and scowled, though my twitching lips ruined the effect. "Are you calling me that horrible name to distract me?"

He chuckled. "I forgot. You hate it when I call you *little*."

"Liar," I accused. "You know very well I hate it when you use that term. Now, answer my question. Are you teasing me to try and distract me?"

He leaned in closer until his mouth nearly touched mine. I felt his warm breath feather across my lips as he spoke. "I was considering distracting you in a different way."

"What did you have in mind?" I asked in a breathy voice.

"This one," he whispered before he kissed me.

His lips moved against mine as I pressed closer to him. My fingers tangled in his soft hair. The magical bond between us hummed and wrapped us in warmth.

"Juliet?"

I pulled back from Dante when I heard Ellis call out my name.

When I looked up, I saw my brother watching us.

His smile was sheepish. "Sorry for interrupting you and your mate when you were going to make a baby."

"Oh, no!" I said quickly. "That's not what we were doing. We were just kissing."

"Yes, just kissing," Dante assured him. "Is everything okay, Ellis?"

He nodded. "Father is awake and asking for you, Juliet."

Dante and I both jumped to our feet and raced toward the cabin.

Chapter Thirty-Three

My father still looked weak, but he was sitting up in bed, and he appeared more lucid. When he saw me, his lips lifted into a shaky smile.

"I was sure I'd only dreamt of seeing you," he said in a raspy voice. "When Ellis told me you were here, I didn't believe him."

"I'm here," I assured him as I sat on the side of his bed.

"How did this happen?" he asked.

"It's a long story that should probably wait until you're feeling better," I told him.

"My mother stuck her in a trap and left her to be killed by spellcasters," Ellis added. "Juliet came back to save you."

"Save me?" my father asked. "Did you find a cure for my illness?"

"You were being poisoned, and yes, I think we cured you," I replied. "Again, this is a very long story, and I promise to tell you everything, but not tonight. We all need our rest. Tomorrow is going to be a very busy day."

"Juliet, I need to know what's going on," he said in a stern tone. "Have you been filling your brother's head with stories about your stepmother? She loves us all and would never hurt a soul.”

“Even now, you doubt me,” I said with a sad sigh.

“What do you expect?” he asked.

“I expect you to believe that Nidia has been lying to you for years,” I told him. “I expect you to believe Ellis and me.”

“It’s true,” Ellis insisted. “Don’t you think it’s strange that my mother said she saw Juliet’s body when Juliet is still alive?”

My father looked at Ellis for several heartbeats before speaking again. “All right. I’ll listen to what you both have to say.”

“We should have more proof for you tomorrow,” I added. “I know you have a lot of questions, but I’m exhausted. We both need rest.”

“Juliet wants to go back outside and kiss her mate again,” Ellis explained.

“Ellis!” I said. “Father doesn’t need to hear about this.”

“What mate?” my father asked.

“You met him earlier,” I reminded him.

His brow creased in concentration. “I think I remember, but it’s all fuzzy. It seemed like a dream. Where is he? I want to see him.”

“You can see Dante tomorrow,” I replied. I’d left Dante outside of the room to avoid discussing my relationship with him until I had more time.

“I don’t know any shapeshifter living in the Heathergate Refuge named Dante,” my father remarked. Though he was trying to sound casual, it came across as suspicious.

I met Ellis’s gaze, hoping he’d take the hint and not reveal too much more information.

“He’s the one who saved Juliet,” Ellis announced.

My father’s lips lifted into a smile, and he closed his eyes. “Well, then I owe this shapeshifter a great debt. I’m looking forward to meeting him tomorrow.”

“Dante is amazing and perfect for me,” I assured him.

My brother wasn’t done raising my father’s curiosity

about Dante. "He helped save your life. Juliet might not have been able to save you without him."

My father's eyes opened again. "He's a healer?"

"No, but he was still able to help, like Serena has," I stated.

My father looked at Serena, who'd moved to the far corner of the room while we spoke.

"She's very kind," he replied.

"Serena saved my life on a different occasion," I told him. "She's my best friend."

"I like her, too," my brother added.

My father gave a slight nod, and his eyes drifted shut again. "Yes, she is a very nice witch. I'll want to hear this story later, Juliet."

My mouth dropped open.

He knew?

His soft snores soon filled the room, and my brother spoke first. "I thought we were going to be able to surprise him by telling him Serena is a witch. He always knows what's going on."

I let out a sad sigh as I looked at our father. "If that was true, he could have saved everyone a lot of pain."

"I guess you're right," Ellis replied. "Of course, then you wouldn't get to kiss Dante."

"True," I replied with a smile. "This situation is a mess, but I do have Dante and a new best friend."

Serena moved forward. "Everyone needs to get to sleep."

"Yes, we do," I agreed. "Tomorrow is going to be a long day."

Chapter Thirty-Four

The waiting was making me antsy and had been since shortly after we'd arrived at the lake. It was always possible Nidia wouldn't come looking for me, but my gut told me she'd not only come, but that she'd bring her best fighters.

We'd split our forces into three groups. I was by the lake with Dante, Serena, Sin, and the rebel shapeshifters. Only three fighters from the Heathergate Refuge were with us, and they were all out scouting the area. Six had remained behind to guard my father, while the rest of the Heathergate Refuge fighters planned to find Fiona and help subdue any of Nidia's guards who stayed behind.

Thankfully, my shoulder was doing much better that morning.

Alaric approached us in human form. He'd been keeping his distance from Serena to avoid acting irrational. He and Geori had decided to stay in human form for the fight while the other rebels were in wolf form.

"I'm beginning to wonder if we're wasting our time here," he remarked. "It doesn't look like they're coming."

"I think it's too soon to start worrying they won't show up," I told him. "It may take Ellis time to convince his mother that he really saw me, even with Case to back up his story. After that, Nidia will need to gather forces to come out here. We have at least another hour before we should start worrying she's not coming."

"If she won't come to us, then we'll have to go to her," Dante stated.

"Let's hope it doesn't come to that," Serena added. "That would put us in a lot more danger."

"Not to mention endangering my people," I added.

"Our scouts haven't reported back in about twenty minutes. Hopefully, they'll return with news soon," I told the others.

Alaric nodded and looked longingly at Serena for several heartbeats. He shook his head as if to clear it before looking away. "All right. I'll be over with the rest of my people if you need me."

After he walked away, Serena said, "I'm glad he's handling this better."

"We all are," Dante replied. "I'm glad Geori is staying away from you, too."

"I thought you were starting to like Geori more," I remarked.

"It's not a matter of liking him or disliking him," Dante insisted. "I'd prefer to have Alaric more focused, and he acts crazier when Geori is close to Serena."

"It makes me wish you'd found an excuse to leave Alaric behind to guard your father," Serena added.

"I tried to come up with a reason," I told her. "His arguments about needing to lead his people and being good in a fight were sound. Besides, he promised to leave you alone. I told him that if he didn't, you'd turn him into a frog."

"I can't do that," she told me.

"I can," Sin announced cheerfully, having just rejoined us after insisting she needed to go for a swim. "Who do you want turned into a frog?"

"No one, but I told Alaric that Serena would turn him into one if he didn't behave," I replied.

"That would be so much fun!" Sin clapped her hands and bounced up and down.

"Maybe you can turn my stepmother into a frog," I suggested.

"I could," she agreed. "It would use up all of my energy since it's a very difficult spell."

"Then I think we should hold off on that," I replied. "We need you at full strength for any fighting."

"Yes, that's a good idea. I'd rather kill someone than change them into a frog, anyway," she mused. "When will the fighting start? This is getting so boring. I haven't killed anyone since yesterday."

"You've gone longer than that without killing anyone before," Dante reminded her.

"But I thought we'd start killing people as soon as we got here. How long does it take for shapeshifters to make such a short trip?" she complained.

Two large wildcats, both guards on the lookout for Nidia's approach, raced toward us.

"It looks the like our wait is over," I told Sin.

Chapter Thirty-Five

Nidia had around two dozen people with her. She didn't take the lead, probably wanting to decide what kind of threat we posed first. Four guards I only knew in passing stood in front of her. She was also flanked by two guards on each side. The remaining fighters were at the rear.

When she saw that my side was outnumbered, Nidia pushed her way to the front of the group and smirked. "I see you've taken up with the dirty rebels. How did you get them past the protection spell?"

"Does it really matter?" I asked.

"Not really," she replied. "What have you done with your father?"

"My father?" I asked with an innocent bat of my eyes. "Is he missing?"

I stepped forward, with Dante and Serena at my sides.

"Go ahead and play your silly games," she said with a fake laugh. "You'll all be dead soon. That is unless you want to make a deal with me. I don't want to kill you, Juliet. You're like a daughter to me, and I would hate to have to order your torture to get the information I need. Tell me where your father is, and you'll save yourself a lot of pain. I may even let you leave the Heathergate Refuge alive."

"Are you telling me he's not where you left him after

you started poisoning him?" I looked at all of the guards with her. "Why are you following this traitor who would murder your leader?"

"Stupid child! Why should anyone listen to you?" Nidia's attention moved around the others with me. "Did Juliet tell you she has a history of making up horrible stories about me because she's jealous of my relationship with her father? I tried so hard to be a mother to her, but the foolish girl ran off the first time I tried to take her to the trading post. I don't know what she told you, but it's a lie. Are you willing to die for her? You're outnumbered, and I am offering you freedom. All you have to do is abandon this plot and leave the Heathergate Refuge after you tell me where my mate has been taken."

"Does everyone here know about your attempts to kill my father?" I asked. "Do they all know that you stole my bracelet and left me in a trap to die?"

"These are the types of ugly lies you have told about me since the day your father told you he loved me," she accused with righteous indignation. I began to wonder if she'd started to believe her own lies. "You hate that he always loved me more than your mother and that he would have been much happier with your brother as his heir. Do your *friends* here know about your mother's dirty little secret?" An evil laugh escaped her lips. "I'll bet you don't even know the truth."

"I know the truth," I replied with a sweet smile. "And while I'm prepared to step down and allow my brother to become the future ruler, your betrayal will not go unpunished. My father is going to survive, but you won't."

I looked between those surrounding my stepmother as I addressed them. "I am Juliet Shadow Walker. I am descended from both a powerful line of shapeshifters and a powerful line of spellcasters. These are my friends, Dante and Serena Verdugo. If you choose to remain loyal to my stepmother, you will die. It's not just my spellcaster friends you have to worry about. I also have shapeshifters who are willing to fight with me. They know the truth of who I am, and they are loyal to me. What will it be? Will you die?"

I was glad I'd told the Heathergate Refuge fighters about my spellcaster heritage the night before. Though I hadn't been certain, I'd suspected Nidia would use it to try to convince the shapeshifters to abandon me.

"Don't be fools!" Nidia shouted at her guards. "It's much too late to change sides. Do you honestly think this little mutt won't kill you? Do you think her father won't order your deaths for betraying him? She's lying."

I shrugged. "I'm not saying everyone will escape punishment, but you are much more likely to survive my father's wrath if you abandon Nidia and her rebellion."

Nidia snorted. "Your father will be dead soon. What makes you think anyone here sees him as a threat?"

"You're wrong," Dante argued. "I've given her father a healing spell. He's recovering and will be ready to take his revenge very soon. We've told him of your betrayal."

"Time's running out to save yourselves," Serena said with a sweet smile.

I could see that several among Nidia's ranks were starting to have their doubts. Likely, some were so deeply involved they knew there was no way their lives would be spared, but others seemed to be weighing their options. Though I was fairly confident we could win in the fight against the shapeshifters, I still preferred to even up the odds and avoid as much risk to my friends as possible.

"My friend is right," I agreed. "Time is running out. You all know my father is a fair man, and he will look more kindly on those who side with me today."

"This cause isn't worth dying for," one of Nidia's guards called out from behind her as he moved to the side.

The one directly to Nidia's left gestured to us as he spoke. "Don't you see? This proves Juliet is dangerous. She let rebel shapeshifters in without gaining permission from the leadership council. She probably stole bracelets for them."

"Her father found a way to bring a spellcaster into the Heathergate Refuge and pass her off as one of ours!" Nidia shouted. "You can't trust him after he lied to your leadership council."

The leadership council had been one of the things that made it hardest for me to believe my uncle's story about my mother. My father had final say on matters, but I doubted he would have brought my mother in without notifying the council. They kept records of every member of the Heathergate Refuge. My father could have convinced many that my mother was a member of an outlying family, but not the council members.

"That's a lie," I accused. "How can any of you think our leadership council wouldn't have questioned my mother's appearance here? Nidia wouldn't have needed a convoluted plan to remove me as next in line to lead if the council hadn't already known about my mixed heritage. All she'd have needed to do was tell them of my father's deception."

Nidia cast quick glances at the guards around her, and I could see her rising panic. Some of them had already abandoned her cause, and others were starting to question what they'd been told.

"Kill them all!" she shouted. "Kill everyone not loyal to me!"

Chapter Thirty-Six

Only four among Nidia's ranks abandoned her cause. I didn't need to give the order; Alaric and the other rebel shapeshifters jumped into the fray to help the guards who were now fighting on our side.

The five guards near the front raced toward us; two held dart guns while the others were armed with small swords. Nidia had been a fool for keeping everyone in human form. She likely believed the weapons would make up for what they lacked in speed, but she'd underestimated the rebel shapeshifters.

Sin held back, but I trusted she'd join the fight when needed, or when she was ready, whichever came sooner.

Nidia edged away from the fighting between the rebels and her guards. Dante and Serena first took down the guards holding dart guns and then focused on the three with swords.

Since everything seemed to be under control, I ran after my stepmother when she made a break for it. I couldn't let her leave the area and possibly sound the alarm with the other traitors.

Nidia was much taller and a faster runner, so I was worried I'd lose her. We were some distance from the fighting when her pace slowed.

There were several trucks a short distance away, and I needed to get to her before she reached one. My lungs burned, and my legs ached as I pushed myself to run faster. Once I was close enough, I leaped forward and tackled Nidia.

Desperate to get away, she shrieked and reached back to claw at my face.

She was still out of breath when she started making threats. "I will kill you myself."

When I pulled back to avoid a jab of her elbow, she scrambled out from under me and landed a kick to my face. She tackled me and wrapped her fingers around my throat.

Reaching up, I clawed at her wrists to try to pry her hands off my neck, but her fingers just tightened.

A maniacal laugh escaped her lips and sent spittle flying into my face. "You'll be dead soon, and then I'm going to find your father and kill him. You should have stayed away from here and been grateful I let you live."

I clawed at her wrists and tried bucking her off, but it did no good. It was tempting to draw on Dante's magic, but I didn't want to weaken him unless I had no other choice.

"You'll never find my father without my help," I gasped out. "He'll survive and destroy you. I already told him you were poisoning him."

She loosened her hold on my throat.

"Tell me where he is, and I'll let you live," she promised.

I whispered nonsense and then let out a soft sob.

"Speak up!" she hissed, further loosening her hold on my throat.

When my next words were quieter still and more garbled, she was foolish enough to lean forward to better hear what I was saying. I grabbed the back of her hair tightly and pulled her down to slam my forehead into her nose.

She screamed and tried to pull away as tears and blood poured down her face.

"I'll kill you!" she screeched, but it was too late.

I shoved her off, got to my feet, and jumped back.

"You'll pay for this," she snarled as she tried standing.

I kicked her chin, and Nidia's head snapped back. She fell to the ground and didn't move again.

"Very nice!" Sin praised as she approached me from behind.

"What are you doing here?" I asked. "I thought you'd stay behind to help the others."

She shrugged from my side. "They had everything under control, and I was worried about you when I saw two traitors follow you. Don't worry. I killed them. I was really hoping you'd need my help. I'd like to destroy your stepmother."

I was tempted to ask her to do it. I'd initially planned to kill Nidia but decided against it. She could help by identifying her fellow traitors, and I also hoped to find out exactly what kind of poison my father had been given.

"You want me to do it, don't you?" Sin sounded thrilled with the idea.

"Yes," I admitted with a sigh. "She deserves to die, but that will have to wait. We may need her. Can you help me get her secured?

Sin pouted for a moment before nodding. "Fine, I'll help you tie her up. I can always destroy her later."

Dante jogged toward us as we transported my stepmother to the back of one of the trucks. He didn't look overly worried, likely because he could sense I was okay through our link. That was why I hadn't rushed back to check on him. I'd have felt his pain if he was injured and his distress if one of our friends were seriously injured.

"You didn't kill her?" he asked.

"I offered to do it for her," Sin told him as she shut the back of the truck.

"We still need answers," I explained.

He nodded. "Good thinking. We kept as many of the traitors alive as possible for that reason."

I threw myself into his arms and held him close. "I can't believe this whole nightmare is nearly over. Well, at least the part about saving my people.”

He pulled away and flashed me a wry smile. “Yes, there is still the matter of Serena and my death sentences.”

“I don’t know if we’ll be able to stay here, so we may need to find a new place to live,” I added. “For now, let’s enjoy this victory.”

“Yes,” he agreed. “We should check to see if we’ve received any messages from Case.”

“And let him know we were successful,” I added. “That should help loosen the tongues of any who still think Nidia is going rescue them.”

He caught my hand and brought it to his lips. “And then maybe we can just enjoy being together for a few minutes.”

I leaned into his side. “I plan to enjoy a lifetime of being with you.”

Epilogue

My father's recovery took several weeks, which came as no surprise to the healers treating him. They all said it was a miracle he was still alive. Without the intervention of spellcasters, my father would be dead, and nearly everyone at the Heathergate Refuge was happy he was alive.

Sadly, their joy didn't translate to them welcoming Dante and Serena with open arms. They were also less than welcoming of the rebel shapeshifters.

Though I'd told Alaric and the other rebels they could return home whenever they wanted, all had decided to stay at least until things were settled at the Heathergate Refuge.

They might change their minds since it didn't look like things would be settled any time soon. For now, I was grateful to have my friends with me, especially since I felt so disconnected from my old life.

Ellis had been vocal about extending a welcome to all rebel shapeshifters and even demanded we do more to reach out to them.

My brother was quite eloquent for a nine-year-old. I no longer had any doubts he'd be a good leader. It hadn't been discussed yet, but I was beginning to feel that it was Ellis's destiny and not mine. It wasn't about me not wanting to lead so much as realizing my people weren't ready to fully accept a half-spellcaster, especially not one bound to a former hunter.

"You look deep in thought," Dante remarked from my side.

We were all sitting in my father's home, waiting for him to return from his meeting with the leadership council. They'd agreed to offer us temporary sanctuary with no promise for how long that would last.

After my father felt up to taking over his duties again, he said we could stay as long as we wanted. Since a decision of that magnitude would normally be run by the council, they hadn't reacted well to his declaration. He might have the final say, but the council expected to have input.

I'd reminded him that acting like a tyrant without considering his people's feelings might not be the best way to keep the peace after the recent attempt to remove him from power. There were clearly those who weren't happy, and he needed to tread lightly. He'd reluctantly agreed to let the leadership council decide if we could stay.

We all expected to be sent away.

"Where are we going when they kick us out?" Serena asked.

"You can all come with us," Geori offered.

"I'm not sure we'll be welcomed back," I replied.

"Sure you will," Alaric insisted. "You're trying to arrange for some of us to live here and to bridge the gap between our people. You and your brother have already changed a lot of minds. I'm sure you'll be welcome among my people."

Elena let out a bark of laughter. "Liar!"

"I won't let my friends be turned away," Alaric insisted.

"You can always go to Reaper Ridge," Sin added.

"Pops didn't seem to think they'd welcome me back," Dante reminded her.

"I can make it happen," Sin argued.

"See?" I told the others. "There's nothing to worry about. We have options."

"Yet you still look worried," Dante pointed out.

"Maybe a little," I agreed.

My father entered the room, cursing under his breath. "Stupid, bigoted council."

"It's okay," I assured him. "They're probably more paranoid than usual, and this is a lot to spring on them. We'll go so you don't have to fight the council."

He shook his head. "They aren't banishing you, but they're still uneasy. We've come to an agreement. You can set up a small community and welcome in up to twenty rebel shapeshifters. The spellcasters can stay, but there will be no more of their kind allowed into the Heathergate Refuge. They were reluctant to make this concession."

"We can have our own community here?" I asked.

He nodded. "By the lake. They won't even consider allowing you to remain my heir now that you've taken a spellcaster as your mate. I can override that decision, but not without some problems."

I hugged him. "Don't push the issue. This is great news!"

He pulled back and scowled. "How is this good news? You were meant to be the ruler of the Heathergate Refuge."

I shook my head. "No, that's a better role for Ellis. I'm going to be your liaison to the rebels."

He let out a sigh. "You would make a good leader, but I suppose your brother will as well, especially with you to support him." His attention shifted to Dante. "I appreciate all you've done for my daughter and for me."

"I love her," Dante replied simply. "Juliet is my other half."

My father laughed. "Other half? Is he always this much of a romantic?"

I flashed Dante a fond smile. "Yes, and he's absolutely perfect for me."

"We're perfect for each other," Dante replied.

"Enough of that, you two," Serena interrupted. "We

need to plan our new homes."
    "Yes, it's time to plan our new beginning," I agreed.

Author's Note

I hope you are enjoying this new world. After writing Dante and Juliet's story, there is still so much to explore. I have big plans for Serena. Who will she end up? As I finished writing this last book, even I didn't know.

Authors and readers rely on reviews, so please take a moment to review this book.

About the Author

Born and raised in the San Francisco Bay Area, C.L. Bright is a hard-working homeschooling mom who loves music, cooking, and reading. Even with her busy schedule, she still manages to find time to explore her artistic side by writing tales of unique worlds.

A few middle school typing classes sparked her obsession with writing and launched her creative adventures. Since then, she has devoted herself to exploring the art of storytelling. For several years, she used a pseudonym to write adult romantic novels. When her writing piqued the interests of her daughters, she decided to venture into the young adult genre so they can also enjoy her books.

Ingram Content Group UK Ltd.
Milton Keynes UK
UKHW022245220623
423898UK00014B/1627